BLYTHE
THE TRAILER PARK KNIGHT RISES

DAN WICKLINE

DARK MUSE PRESS

Cover art by: Phillip Sevy

Edited by: Tim Dedopulos

Published by: Dark Muse Press

Visit the author website: www.danwickline.com

Version 2018.12.01

DEDICATION

To Lisa – This whole thing started because of our conversation on the ride home from the Phoenix Comic Con and you asking where we were. Just another example of how you inspire me.

Also from Dan Wickline

For more of Dan's work visit:
www.danwickline.com

ACKNOWLEDGMENTS

This is a private printing of the novel. Only twenty-five copies printed and giving to those that not only helped make this book happen, but helped to make me a writer. If this book is in your hand then you have helped inspire me and I appreciate having you in my life.

CHAPTER ONE

Erin took a knee next to the large-nosed garden gnome holding the make-shift mushroom rake. The coarse, white gravel on the ground around it pushed against her kneecap in a most unpleasant way. She was amazed at how the jagged little edges could find the tiny gaps in the padding she wore. She pushed the thought of that out of her mind and focused on the task at hand.

The last trailer in the park sat alone in the far back corner. It had to be over forty years old and whatever color it had been in the beginning was long faded away into a mix of gray and rust. It was a good fifty yards from any other trailer. Robert had told her it wasn't always this way, but once the park changed hands, the new owner allowed this trailer to move in and everyone around it began to leave if they could. Even when you're poor and desperate, you don't want to live too close to a meth lab. The residents feared the people who worked in the trailer and the possibility of an accident. Robert said at least a dozen people had made calls to the police, but not a single squad car came out.

Robert was frustrated. His neighbors were scared. Erin could think of no reason not to get involved. She didn't have a job, a family or anything close to a future. If it wasn't for Robert letting her crash on his couch, she wouldn't even have a roof over her head. She figured the least she could do was scare off a couple of drug dealing morons.

She'd planned it out the night before while having a few beers, her ideas getting better as the 12-pack got empty. She then had the full morning to think of a reason not to, but found none. She waited for the sun to go down and squeezed into her old wetsuit, one of the few things she found in her father's storage unit. The suit still fit but only barely. There was some disconcerting tugging when she moved in certain ways. On top of that she put on the old black and gold paintball gear she'd found in Robert's storage shed — a pair of knee and elbow pads, a chest guard and a face mask. She added her own combat boots. She looked for something to put over her short, blond hair, but nothing she could find would work with the mask.

She quickly got bored with looking and decided to just go for it. She took his paintball gun and holster for effect. She found a pair of rattan escrima sticks she wrapped in black electrical tape and slid in between the back of the chest guard and her wetsuit. She thought she looked bad-ass.

Robert said he only ever saw one guy there at night. Erin figured she could sneak up to the place, smack the guy around until he ran off, then mess up the lab a little causing them to find another location. It'd seemed like a good plan the night before. She could see the flaw though. Hard to sneak up over a 50-yard distance. Nothing to cover her approach except for an old pickup with a camper on the back. It was parked next to the trailer. She realized she could approach from an angle that kept the truck between her and the trailer. She liked this new plan. Had a lot of confidence in it. She gulped down the last of her beer, pulled the hard-plastic visor mask down over her face and followed the row of trailers to the left until she was in perfect line with the pick-up.

Other than tripping over the cinderblock brick that someone had left in the dirt, falling face first and smashing her mask against her nose, making it bleed, the approach to the truck went perfectly. There was even a bandana hanging on the antenna she was able to use to clean up the blood on her face. Her nose didn't feel broken, but she wasn't sure if that meant it wasn't or the beer had dulled the pain. Either way, the plan was still moving forward, and she saw a way to improve it.

Instead of just walking up to the door of the trailer, she thought about going up on the roof and dropping in through a vent. Like in the comics when the hero dropped through the skylight. It always surprised the bad guys and Erin knew surprise would be a good thing. She could climb up the hood of the truck, got on top of the camper and step over to the roof of the trailer. She felt this was a brilliant modification to the plan.

She used the front tire as a step and got onto the hood. From there she pulled herself up the side of the overhead bed space and onto the top of the camper. She completed this move without making a single sound, other than the curse word when her chest guard got caught on the side window and she had to struggle a minute to get loose. Other than that, it was flawless execution. She flopped over onto her back and listened for movement. For a second she regretted not bringing another beer, then reminded herself she didn't have any pockets on her outfit.

She got up onto her knees and looked over at the trailer. It seemed quiet, other than a song playing from a radio inside. If you would've asked Erin what music would be playing in a meth lab a few hours earlier, she probably would've said some classic rock like Leonard Skynard or the Eagles. Maybe even some Black Sabbath. What she heard coming through the air vents of the ancient trailer was the unmistakable wailings of Fred Schneider of the B-52's singing about a Rock Lobster. She hated that song with all the fiery passions of Hell. Had she not already planned on going in there and smacking the guy around, she would definitely be going in there and smacking the guy around.

She glanced over to the other roof. From a distance, it seemed like the camper was parked right next to the trailer. From here she could clearly see that it was more like five feet away. A jump she was more than capable of making, but not silently. She would need to land close to the air vent and drop through quickly before losing the element of surprise. She tugged the paintball gun out of its holster, figuring having it in hand when she dropped in would be extra intimidating.

She took a few steps back, then started towards the trailer. After two full strides she leapt across the open space just as Fred belted out, "Boys in Bikinis!" She was thinking how much she hated that song as her boot made contact with the metal roof of the trailer, and broke through. She fell into the trailer with a thud. Pieces of debris rained down around her. A clump of asbestos insulation clung to her visor.

The man inside the trailer let out a string of curse words and backed away quickly. Though it was hard to move quickly in a trailer full of boxes. It was exactly the effect Erin was hoping for. The part she wasn't happy about was that he had a friend who wasn't spooked at all. Instead he drew a Glock model 40 and pointed it at her.

"Don't shoot!" the cook yelled. "This place will blow sky high!"

The guy with the gun hesitated for just a second. Erin didn't. She fired her weapon and a small gelatin capsule struck the main in the bridge of his nose. The projectile burst open and a spray of gold paint blanketed his eyes, blinding him. His free hand shot up to try and clear his vision.

Erin reached back for her escrima sticks, but found herself being pummeled by a barrage of various small items — bags of meth, scissors, a half-eaten McDonald's Filet-O-Fish. The cook was literally throwing everything at her. It wasn't doing any damage, but it was annoying as hell. She picked up a hammer that was lying on the counter next to her and hurled it at him. He ducked out of the way, but proceeded to hit his forehead on the door, stunning himself for a minute.

By then the gunman had gotten enough paint out of his eyes to see his target, and charged her. She hadn't seen him move and was caught off guard. His shoulder hit her in the chest and lifted her up off her feet. His momentum drove them back into the wall. Being crushed between his shoulder and the wall pushed all the air out of her lungs. She couldn't catch her breath. And he drove his knee up into her stomach.

Pain shot through her body and her lungs burned. He was too close for her to punch with any force, so she slammed her forehead down into the gold painted bridge of his nose. Her mask jammed against her face and she could feel her nose start to bleed again, but the strike worked. He staggered back away, clutching his shattered nose. She stepped forward and drove the toe of her combat boot up into his groin. As he doubled over in pain, she brought the knee of her other leg up hard into his chin. He flew back into the cooking area, sending everything flying.

"Jesus Christ!" the cook shouted. "What have you done!"

Erin glanced over to where the gunman had landed and saw that a fire had started and was growing fast. The cook helped the gunman to his feet. Remarkably the guy had not dropped his gun through any of it. The cook was pulling him towards the door, but he was bringing the gun around towards Erin. He got off three rounds before being pulled out the door.

She had been shot at before and Erin knew the best way to stay alive was to not be in the same place when the bullets showed up. She had already started towards the floor before the first shot was fired. She heard the door slam and knew they were gone. The fire was spreading quickly and though she knew almost nothing about meth, she did know that meth labs can blow up in spectacular fashion. She scrambled to her feet and got to the door. It wouldn't budge. They'd jammed something up against it. She turned to look for the door at the other end, the fire blocked her path. She looked around for any other avenues of escape, then remembered she had already made one.

She jumped up onto the counter and reached for the edge of the hole she created with her entrance, hoping the metal was strong enough to support her while she pulled herself up. It held as she made her way onto the trailer roof. Not hesitating for an instant, she quickly leapt over to the top of the camper then jumped down onto the hood of the pickup, and then onto the ground. She glanced around for a second to see where the two guys had gone. She didn't want to suddenly be shot after her daring escape from the burning trailer. They were nowhere in sight.

Not knowing how long she had, she sprinted for the line of regular trailers. The ill-fitting pads shifting as she ran. She could taste the blood from her nose as it had covered her mouth and was sucked in with each breath. Twenty yards away, was that far enough she thought? She couldn't risk being wrong and kept running.

The sound wasn't what she expected. Just a giant, "Whummm", and then she was hit by a tsunami wave of force, hurling her like a rag doll until she slammed into the side of a blue and white trailer thirty feet from where she had started. She heard things crack and wasn't sure which sounds were her hard-plastic gear and which were he bones. But it didn't stop with the impact. She felt the force of the blast continuing to push her against the steel wall as if it wouldn't stop until she passed through to the other side.

And suddenly it was gone. She tumbled to the ground. Not backwards, but somehow twisting as she fell so her face hit first and the metal end of a garden hose jammed into her chest. She wanted nothing more than to move it, but her brain and her limbs weren't on speaking terms at that moment. She laid there for an eternity, or a few seconds. She wasn't sure which it was. Finally, she shook the rattling in her brain long enough to hear a repeating sound.

Cheet. Cheet. Cheet. Cheet.

She willed her head to turn and it grudgingly obliged. She looked up and saw an elderly man wearing a robe, slippers and nothing else. She knew the last part because of the upward angle she was looking at him from. He held a cell phone and continue taking pictures.

"Hello…" she said weakly.

"Oh good. You're not dead." The old man snorted. "Mind getting off my petunias?"

Erin glanced down and saw a line of flowers on either side of her and realized she was likely crushing two or three. Her body was sorer than she could remember it ever being, but she didn't think anything was broken. Or at least she hoped nothing was. She slowly got to her feet, letting her body adjust to each movement before starting the next.

The old man had stopped taking pictures of her and was focusing on what was left of the meth lab. "You know, I personally called the police four times about them. Not once did they bother to show up. A shame it took an accident like this to get them to finally come out."

Erin wasn't sure what he meant. "Accident?"

"Well, I can't speak for everyone here, but I sure didn't see anything. Must've been an accident." He tucked his phone away. "I think I hear sirens in the distance. You better vanish, youngster."

Her ears were still ringing, so she couldn't make out the sirens, but she took the man's advice anyway. She started back to Robert's trailer but then saw the first flashes of red and blue lights coming through the front gate. She immediately turned to the right and ran as fast as her beat-up body could towards the side fence.

She had found a spot a few weeks ago where the chain links had been cut and she could squeeze through to the self-storage place the next lot over. This came in handy as her father's storage unit was near there and she could easily go back and forth instead of going out and around through the front gates.

She made her way through the rows of units until she found the right one. It was a combination lock, her birthday. He told her that in the last letter he wrote to her while she was deployed. It took her two tries, but she got it open, rolled up the big metal door and then pulled it down behind her. There was a battery-operated lantern right where she had left it. She flicked it on and the blue-white light filled the ten by twenty unit. There wasn't much left in it, but there was a sleeping bag and some of her old clothes. Both would be helpful.

She pulled off the mask and found a rag to wipe up the blood on her face. There was a half-finished bottle of water from her last trip that she used to clear her mouth. She then pulled off the chest guard, the pads and the boots. Her body felt like she had tumbled down a steep hill in a barrel full of rocks. She squeezed out of the wetsuit and saw various patches of discoloration across her arms and chest that were a promise of massive bruises to come. Half-naked, she slipped into the sleeping bag, bundled up the wet suit as a pillow and turned off the lantern.

She laid I the dark, trying to figure out why she had done something so stupid and missing her father.

CHAPTER TWO

"What the hell were you thinking?!"

The words poured into her ear like they were shot from a fire hose, but still her sleeping mind deemed it unimportant enough to bring the rest of her back to consciousness. She had woken up after a few hours in the storage unit, found a pair of jeans and t-shirt, then headed back to the hole in the fence. Once she was sure that the police had cleared out, she made her way back to Robert's trailer. She let herself in quietly and sprawled out on the couch like she did every night. She was sure that Robert hadn't seen her leave, so no one would know what she'd done.

"Wake up, you idiot!"

Those words registered a little more with her brain. At least the last word. She really didn't like being called an idiot, or stupid. Without even opening her eyes, she shot her foot out towards the voice. The heel of her foot connected with something metal, like a thin pole, and it shot away from her as soon as she hit it. Then she heard a loud thud, followed by cursing. Those words made her sleeping mind retreat and allowed consciousness to take over.

"Son of bitch!"

Erin quickly spun up to a seated position, her eyes wide and her muscles ready to move. But what she saw was her friend, Robert Alvarez, lying on the floor, his cane kicked halfway across the room and him looking at her with anger in his eyes. She immediately jumped to her feet and retrieved his cane. She handed it to him and then tried to help him up. He jerked his arm away from her.

"Don't touch me!" Robert struggle to his feet.

He was wearing a pair of boxers and a t-shirt. He didn't go around that often without his prosthetic leg. This was only the third or fourth time she'd seen him without it. Her mind flashed back to that mission in Afghanistan, the mission where everything had gone south. She tried not to think about it as it tended to pull her in deep. Sometimes she couldn't help it.

"What the hell were you thinking?!"

Erin snapped out of it and looked at Robert again. He was still angry, but he was holding out his computer tablet to her. She took it and glanced down at the screen. It was the front page of the Palo Verde Valley Times, the only thing the city of Blythe had close to a local newspaper. The headline read, "Drug Lab Blown Up By Trailer Park Vigilante." Underneath that was a photo of her running towards the camera as the lab blew up behind her. It was quite an impressive shot, like something out of a Hollywood movie.

"Wow, that looks intense. I wonder…"

"Stop!" Robert held up his hand. "Before you even begin the lie, let me point out that you are a horrible liar, I recognize my own paintball gear and the explosion woke me and everyone else in the park up, and I saw that you weren't here. Would you like to start your answer again?"

Erin swallowed hard. "I was just trying to help."

Robert's expression softened a little and he sat on the arm of the couch. "Why?"

"Because you were constantly complaining about them. How it wasn't safe to live here, but most people couldn't afford to move." She leaned her head back. "I thought I could go over and scare them into relocating. I didn't think it would get so out of hand."

"What went wrong?"

"The plan seemed good when I started." Erin shook her head. "You said there was always one guy at night. I went over there with the idea of smacking him around a bit. But I dropped in and found he had a friend who was quick on the draw. Things went sideways, a fire started and then boom."

Robert shook his head in disbelief. "Did anyone see you?"

"Just Free Willy who took that shot." She looked at the tablet again, scrolled down and saw a picture of her on the petunias, her butt in the main focus of the shot. "I thought the creep was taking pictures of the explosion. At least my ass looked pretty good in the wet suit."

Robert tilted his head and asked, "Who is Free Willy?"

"Old guy in the back row." Erin handed the tablet back. "He was only wearing a robe and from the ground I could see… never mind, it's a long story."

"What?"

Erin blushed a little. "I don't mean he was long. He wasn't exactly short, but I wouldn't call him particularly big either."

Robert threw his hands in the air. "Enough. I don't need an anatomical description of Mr. Johnson. Did he see your face?"

"No." Erin held up her finger. "And when you say, Mr. Johnson, is that his real name or a slang term for a penis?"

"His name is Peter Johnson."

Erin started to snicker. "Of course it is."

Robert hit her in the leg with his cane. "Can you be serious? I want to know if I'm going to have people with guns busting down my door because you got drunk and decided to clean up the park."

"You worried about the cops or the dealers?" Erin sat up straight.

"Both. Hell, in this city, they're probably one and the same." Robert got up and moved over to the window to look outside. "I'm thinking of both our safety here."

"I know you are." Erin stood as well. "I had a mask on the whole time."

"At least you thought that part through." He turned back to her. "You know that there were toxic fumes from the explosion. Luckily the winds were blowing towards the storage units and away from the trailers."

"Oh great. That's where I was." Erin shook her head. "It was stupid. I know. But I can't undo it now."

Robert put his hand on her shoulder. "You had the right intentions. Get rid of the gear, burn it beyond recognition. Lay low and we'll hope that the cops continue their streak of not solving crimes."

"Okay." Erin moved over to the couch where she'd left her cellphone. "I'll cancel my appointment with Hertzberg."

"No!" Robert put his hand over her phone. "You go see the doc."

"You told me to lay low."

"You get to see him once a month if you're lucky. You keep your appointment." Robert put his hand on her shoulder. "Get a shower, I'll make us some breakfast and then I can drop you off on my way to the store."

Erin nodded and headed for the bathroom. She got the water started and closed the door. She stripped off her clothes and looked at herself in the mirror. She had a few new bruises, but nothing that was going to last. Not like the three-inch diagonal scar to the right of her naval or the circular scar between her chest and left shoulder. Those were constant reminders of the past in the same way Robert's missing leg reminded him.

She didn't have any family anymore. No job, no future, and no place to call her own. But she had a friend who was there for her no matter what. And she had just done something stupid that put him at risk. She never would've done that before. She never would've put any of her guys in harm's way. She didn't understand why things had changed so much. Why she couldn't be like she used to be. What happened was horrible and she knew it wasn't her fault. Yet she constantly felt guilty. And angry. The anger was always there, like a boiling pot of water and she can't turn the flame off.

She shook her head. She didn't have time to let the darkness in. She turned and tested the water. The heat stung her skin. Exactly what she wanted. She stepped into the shower and closed the curtain.

Erin sat on a folding chair in the small, non-descript waiting area that had become almost as familiar as the couch at Robert's trailer. Four metal chairs, three of them gray while one was black with chipped off paint and bits of rust. The walls were painted Navajo White and had a rough texture to keep people from touching them. There was a plastic ficus in the corner that even with being fake, still looked like it hadn't been watered in weeks. Other than that, there was nothing to tell you who the waiting room was for, nor even a magazine or pamphlet to pass the time. She'd mentioned that fact to the doctor during their last session. He'd suggested that she should bring something of her own to keep her entertained.

The tennis ball hit the wall for the fourth time when the inner door flew open. Dr. Emile Hertzberg gave her a look of disappointment. Erin flashed back her most innocent, "what do you mean" expression.

"I will be with you in ten minutes. Please keep the noise out here to a minimum," Hertzberg said in a even, patient tone.

"Of course." Erin nodded.

She watched the psychiatrist turn his back and immediately threw the ball at the wall, aiming for a foot to the right of the door. Before the ball hit the wall, Hertzberg's hand shot out and snagged it out of the air. He then dropped it into his pocket and closed the door behind him, never once looking back. Erin made a mental note to bring a superball the following month, then corrected herself. Two superballs.

The ten minutes went by quickly as Erin ran ideas of other annoying things she could do in the waiting room through her mind. Putting fake snails in the fake ficus, gluing down the folding chairs and hanging horror movie posters were a few of her favorites. A smiling old man came out of the doctor's office, put on his driving cap and flipped Erin the bird before leaving. She was about to go after him when Hertzberg called her in.

The office itself wasn't much more opulent than the waiting room. There was a desk in front of the window that looked like it was ordered from the 1947 Sears & Roebuck catalog and an executive office chair that they stacked by the front door at OfficeMart for $59.99. Across from the desk was a pair of faux leather arm chairs in the boxy style that the Swedish seem to love. On the desk was a note pad, a few file folders, a briefcase, the Palo Verde Valley Times and a picture of Mrs. Hertzberg and two little Hertzbergs, one of each gender. The only other thing in the room was a photocopied image of a diploma in a clear plastic frame that was hung on the far wall.

"What's up, Doc?" Erin plopped down in the first of the chairs, leaving her legs hanging over the arm.

"I'm doing well, thank you." Hertzberg's reply was all business. "Catch me up on the last month. Have you made any progress on your goals?"

"You mean did I find a job, my own place or a constructive use of my time? No, no and it really depends on your definition of constructive."

Hertzberg scribbled down a few notes on the pad. "Did you try to find a job?"

"I did." Erin spun in her seat, putting her feet on the floor. "Turns out that neither OfficeMart, Burger Barn nor Payless Food are in need of an employee with Airborne, sniper and unarmed combat training. I even tried to explain the loss prevention potential of having me set up across the street with my Barrett XM109 to catch shoplifters as they exited the building."

"I see that your sarcastic armor is in place." The doctor leaned back in his chair. "You want to tell me what happened, or would you prefer to dance around it for the whole session?"

Erin gave the man a lot of crap, none of it deserved. He was good at his job and if she wasn't trapped out in the middle of nowhere, he might actually be able to help her. But she was living in the black hole of hope and a psychiatric drive-by wasn't going to change that. But the man knew her well enough to see through her bullshit.

She stood up and leaned forward, tapping her finger on the front page of the paper. Hertzberg looked down at the image of the costumed figure and exploding meth lab. The look on his face was one of confusion that slowly changed to realization. He pointed to the picture and then at Erin. She nodded.

"Doctor-patient privilege, right?" Erin asked.

Hertzberg stared at her for a moment before nodding. "Yes. Of course. Whatever you say here is just between you and me."

"That was in the trailer park I'm staying in. I went to scare them off, but things got out of hand." Erin leaned back in her seat again. "I'm not really sure why I did it."

"How did you feel?" Hertzberg steepled his fingers in front of his mouth. "What made you do it?"

"I wanted to help. Robert had been complaining about them for some time and I got the idea that I might be able to do something about it." She looked towards the office door, not wanting to make eye contact. "Honestly, it was the best I've felt in a long time. I wasn't feeling angry or sorry for myself. I wasn't thinking about how fucked up my life is. I just saw something that I could do and did it."

"And now? How do you feel looking back?" He continued to fix his gaze on her.

She turned back and met his gaze. "Guilty. I acted on impulse with a half-ass plan that could've gotten people hurt or killed. I did no recon, made no contingency plans. I went in like a newb and it's my fault the thing blew up."

Hertzberg started quickly scribbling notes and shaking his head. Erin stayed quiet as the doctor wrote, but the silence was starting to make her feel worse.

"And I had been drinking," she admitted.

He nodded at her admission and wrote for a few more second. Then finally, he put his pen down and did the last thing Erin was expecting. He smiled at her.

"Why are you smiling?" Erin was completely confused.

"I have been seeing you for close to a year now, and for the first time in all those sessions I'm seeing the Master Sergeant Erin Cooper that your file describes. The soldier, the leader and the person who is always there for others. I can't condone you taking on a group of drug dealers. But as your psychiatrist this is one of the first positive and healthy things you've done since coming home."

Erin looked dumbfounded. "You're saying this was a good thing?"

Hertzberg put up his hands as he tried to explain. "My concern is your mental health and what you just told me is you did something with the best intentions. Your anger issues weren't a factor and other than beating yourself up for lack of planning, which is due to the alcohol, you actually seem pretty happy with your actions. Am I right?"

She thought about it for a moment. "Yeah. I made the park a bit safer. I do feel good about that."

"I am not in any way suggesting you should continue running around in a…" He glanced at the paper again. "Is that a wetsuit? Anyway. I'm not suggesting you become a vigilante. But you can use your time to help people. Maybe volunteer at a shelter or something. It will help you stay focused while you work on your other goals."

The alarm dinged, signaling that their session was over. Erin stood, not exactly sure how to feel. She'd had no intention of telling the doctor about what happened and when she did, she'd expected him to condemn her actions. Instead he acted like it was a break through and it was all part of his master plan. She headed for the door.

"Hey!"

Erin turned back just in time to catch her tennis ball.

Hertzberg was smiling again. "See you next month."

CHAPTER THREE

Erin caught the bus back to the trailer park and went back to sleep. She still felt exhausted from the night before and hoped a handful of ibuprofen would knock the edge off. She slept until Robert got home at almost four in the afternoon with a bucket of chicken. The smell of the food kicked her hunger into full gear before she even opened her eyes. She sat up and snagged a leg from the buckets as Robert sat it down on the coffee table. He grabbed a couple beers from the fridge and then sat down and joined in on the food. She told him about her visit to the psychiatrist while they ate.

"That's crazy!" Robert accidentally spit out a tiny piece of white meat. "He thinks it was a good idea for you to put on a costume and take on drug dealers?"

Erin shrugged. "I think it was more about my desire to help those around me."

"Where's his degree from, Stan Lee U?" Robert chortled.

After inhaling two more pieces of chicken, Erin slipped her boots back on and looked out the window. The sun was just starting to set.

"You heading out?" Robert started cleaning up the table.

"Going to grab the gear from last night and dump it somewhere." She grabbed her coat and slipped it on. "I was thinking of dropping it in the dumpster behind the gas station on Lovekin."

"The other side of town? Smart." Robert put the half empty bucket in the refrigerator. "I'll drive you."

She waved him off. "Nah. It's a nice night and I could use the walk. Some executive time with my thoughts."

"And if you get stopped by the cops while you're walking?"

She ran the thought through her mind a second. "Let me go get the gear. Be right back."

Robert nodded as Erin opened the door and stepped down into the night. She made her way across the park and cut through the fence again into the storage facility. She did a few passes around to make sure no one was watching her unit before approaching it. Once inside, she found her old high school backpack and shoved the wetsuit and paintball gear into it.

By the time she'd gotten back to the trailer, Robert was getting into his truck. She dropped the backpack into the bed, up against the cab, then slid inside. There were a total of ten stations broadcasting out of Blythe, six of them were religious. One of those being in Spanish. Of the four music stations you had a choice of adult contemporary, country or Spanish. No rock, no metal. Nothing that Erin would want to listen to for more than thirty seconds. Robert had it tuned into a country station where a man sang a song about a plastic drinking cup. She could relate to that.

The drive across town wouldn't take long since what passed for rush hour had already died down. There was no sense hopping on the freeway when they could just head down Hobson Way. Her mind had just begun to wander off when Robert slammed on the brakes. A woman had raced out in front of him more worried about what was behind her than on-coming traffic. Robert just missed her, but others were fleeing across the street as well. Other cars had come to a stop and everyone was looking back at the bank.

It was hard to tell what was going on until a man walked out of the bank carrying an AR-15 rifle. He shot three rounds into the sky above the witnesses and told everyone to leave. People dove behind cars or took off at a run. Panic was taking over for most. Both Erin and Robert had seen worse. The thing that struck Erin as unbelievable was the man wasn't wearing a mask of any kind. He was robbing a bank in full view of everyone like he had no worry in the world of being caught.

"Son of a bitch," Erin growled. "It's him."

Robert glanced over at his passenger. "Who?"

"The other guy from the meth lab." She felt the rage start to build up in her.

"This is your fault then." Robert shook his head.

Erin jerked her head to look at Robert. "How the hell do you figure that?"

"You decided to play hero last night and destroy his lab. He's got bills to pay, maybe owes people for supplies. He's got to make that up." Robert was staring at the man as he went back towards the bank. "Instead of selling drugs to stupid, yet willing clients, he's now down here waving a semi-auto rifle at innocent people because you thought you'd help out. This is definitely your fault."

"You're right." Erin had the door open and was out of the cab before Robert could even move. "I should've put them both down and been done with it."

She tossed her coat into the back and had the chest piece out of the backpack and over her t-shirt in the blink of an eye. She slid on the mask, grabbed the escrima sticks and turned back towards the bank.

"What do you think you're doing? This is crazy!" Robert yelled at her.

She turned and looked back for just a moment. "Go home."

The gunman was back in the bank and not looking at the street when Erin made her determined walk towards the front door. In her mind she knew this was suicide. She wasn't even trying to sneak in. She walked straight forward, a stick in each hand. She could hear the crowd starting to whisper. She made out the words newspaper and explosion, but didn't really care. She was angry. Angrier than she'd been in a very long time. She had tried to do something to help people. Clean up the park for Robert and the other residents. But it wasn't enough. The bad guys would just go on and hurt someone else. Why was the world so fucking unfair?

Erin was three feet from the door when the gunman looked up and saw her. He pushed the door open, swinging the gun out in front of him. But he chose the wrong door. Instead of the door opening toward her, he took the door closest to her that opened away. She raced forward, slamming her shoulder into the door, causing the man to stagger back and the rifle to get trapped between the two doors as she kept her weight against the one. She then swung one of the sticks down as hard as she could on to his wrist. It loosened the man's grip just enough that when she yanked the door out towards her, the rifle fell to the ground.

The man reached down for the weapon, but his eyes were locked on Erin's mask. "Oh shit."

The first swing of the stick caught the man in the left temple. The second slammed into the bridge of his nose with the snapping sound of breaking a cookie in half. The third strike was across the chin and the man went stumbling backwards. The strikes were so quick, he hadn't even had a chance to raise his hands to block before he found himself tripping into the bank and leaving a trail of blood.

Erin hadn't chosen the escrima sticks because they were there or would look good with the outfit. She picked them because she had been using them her whole life. Her father taught her how to use them when she was seven. Her friends were learning to twirl batons or flags, Erin could roll through the Heaven 6 like it was a ballet dance.

The man steadied himself, spun and charged towards her, hands reaching out to grab her. She brought the left stick down hard across his wrists as she sidestepped the lunge. She then thrust her right knee up into his exposed solar plexus, doubling him over as the air shot out of his lungs.

She finished up with a crack to the back of his head with the right stick. He slammed face first down to the ground, unconscious.

"Jesus Christ, lady! What did we do to piss you off?" A shaky voice from over Erin's shoulder called out.

She turned slowly to find the cook from the meth lab holding a .38 revolver pointed at her. But pressed against him was a very scared looking Asian woman with tears streaming out from under her glasses. They were about fifteen feet away from her. Too far to rush and keep him from getting a shot off. And with the way his arm was shaking, he would fire the moment she moved.

She needed to calm him down. "What do you mean?"

"You came after us last night, and now you're here again." He moved the gun as he talked, gesturing with it. "Did we sell you bad shit or something?"

"I was just driving by. Didn't know it was you," Erin lied.

"What is it then? You some kind of vigilante?" He loosened his grip on the woman just a little. "Like in the comic books."

Erin had no idea why, but the guy seemed to relax with this line of thinking. That she wasn't after him personally. She needed to keep him talking, so she looked around the room for inspiration. That's when she saw the sign for the Palo Verde High Hornets football team. They wore black and gold, the same as the gear she had on.

"Just like that. I'm called The Sting." She said the last part with as much emphasis as she could muster.

"Like the singer?" The guy looked confused.

"No!" She shook her head. "Like the attack of a hornet."

The hostage looked between the gunman and the masked woman and seemed to understand what Erin was trying to do. She nervously chimed in. "That's a good name. You know a hornet's sting is more painful to humans than a wasp's stings because a hornet's venom contains a large amount of acetylcholine."

The cook looked down at the woman. "Really? How do you know?"

"Entomology is a hobby of mine." She gave a shy smile. "There's a lot of cool insects in this area."

"I was always fascinated with ants when I was a kid." The cook turned to look at the woman, letting her go completely and ignoring Erin now. "Jimmy—he's over there on the floor—he always wanted to burn them with a magnifying glass. But I liked to try and dig into their hills and see all the tunnels and stuff."

The cook turned to face the hostage, swinging his gun in her direction. The woman's eyes went wide as the barrel kept swinging back and forth in front of her chest as the man talked. She gave a half smile at him while her fearful eyes seemed to plead for help.

Erin quietly moved across the room as he talked. When she got close enough, she sprang forward, grabbing his wrist and forcing the gun into the air. He was about to protest when she tapped the side of his face with one of her sticks.

"You can just give me the gun and I won't have to hit you." She tapped again. "Or we can take the painful route. I'm good either way."

The guy sighed, handed her the gun and then dropped down onto his knees, putting his hands behind his head.

"I appreciate the option," he admitted.

Erin looked around as the other people in the bank started getting to their feet. She could hear sirens getting closer and noticed a guy in a suit approaching.

"I'm Mr. Wilkes, the bank manager." He reached out his hand and shook Erin's. "Thank you, Miss Sting, for dealing with this situation so efficiently."

"Don't mention it." She handed him the gun. "But I need to go before the cops see me."

Wilkes reaches into his pocket and pulls out some keys. "Blue Honda Civic out back. Just call the bank tomorrow and let me know where you leave it. Put the keys under the seat, I have a spare."

Erin was stunned for a moment, then took the offered car keys. "Thank you."

She headed for the door and noticed a few people smiling and waving to her as she passed.

"Oh, ma'am." Mr. Wilkes called out. "There are cameras in the parking lot, so don't take your mask off until you're well clear of the building."

She nodded to him then exited the building. She moved quickly around the side and found the car in the back corner of the lot. She slid in and the engine fired up on the first try. She needed to adjust the seat, but that could wait until she was on the move. She pulled out of the bank parking lot slowly, not wanting to draw attention to herself. She could see the squad car pulling up in her rear-view mirror as she made it through the first signal. That's when she pulled off her mask and tossed it on the passenger seat.

Her hands were shaking from the adrenaline. She knew what she'd just done was crazy, but she felt good. The best she had in years. She stopped a bank robbery, and no one got hurt. Okay, Willy got hurt. But Willy had a gun and was one of the guys doing the robbery, so him getting hurt was okay. No innocent people got hurt. She didn't get hurt. How could this not be a good thing?

Then she remembered why she went in there in the first place. It wasn't to help people—she was pissed off. How could those guys be out robbing a bank right after she took out their meth lab? And Erin realized Robert was right. They were out robbing the bank because she took out their meth lab. As much as she thought she was doing a good thing, all those people at the bank were put at risk because of her.

She drove to the gas station on Lovekin and tossed the mask, chest piece and sticks into the dumpster as she had originally planned. She drove about halfway back home, a couple blocks from the bank and left the Honda, tucking the keys under the seat. She then walked the half mile down the street to the Karma Chameleon. She found Robert sitting at his usual bar stool, nursing a beer. She walked up and stood near him.

"I'm sorry," she said in a soft voice.

He looked into her eyes for a moment, then gestured to the empty stool next to him. As she sat down, Robert raised his hand and signaled to the bartender. Connie, who knew what everyone drank without asking, popped open another beer and placed it down in front of Erin. She picked it up and felt the cool chill against her hand. She leaned it out towards her friend, who clinked it with his own bottle, and they both drank.

As she drank her beer, she was thinking about what she would tell Dr. Hertzberg on their next visit. That she had indeed started out trying to help, something he saw as a positive, but her anger once again took over. Maybe he'd be impressed that she was able to recognize it before it got too out of hand. He always said that recognizing that you have a problem was the first step. She needed to introduce positive things into her life, build towards a secure future and work on controlling her anger. Putting on a mask and beating the crap out of bad guys was not a positive thing. No matter how good it felt. And it seriously felt good.

CHAPTER FOUR

Rock Carrington guided his 2009 Cadillac CTS into his reserved parking spot in front of City Hall. He clicked off the satellite radio just as Neil Diamond started singing about Sweet Caroline. He would've stayed a few minutes and listened if he wasn't already late. And this was one of those meetings he definitely didn't want to miss. He spread the sun visor out across his dashboard. The car was almost nine years old, but the interior still looked new thanks to proper care and maintenance. He grabbed his leather satchel off the passenger seat. He missed the days of having a brief case, but Audrey told him that the satchel made him look more with the times. And she would know better than him. As he opened his door her found one of the faces he truly hated waiting for him.

"Mayor Carrington! Bernie Greene, Blythe Bulletin!" A nasally voice called out from the hood of the car.

"I know who you are, Bernie." Carrington closed the door and chirped the lock. "You're fake news."

"Just because you don't like the questions doesn't mean you get to attack the fourth estate," Green countered. "The press is duty bound to ask the tough questions."

"But you're not the press." Carrington walked straight up to the reporter and glared down at him. "You don't work for television, radio or even a newspaper. You write a blog that on your best day gets a hundred hits. And that's when you're posting your Aunt Myrtle's recipes. You're not real news. Go away."

Carrington, who stood six inches taller than Green and had him beat by at least seventy-five pounds, glowered at the man until the reporter took a step back. The mayor then turned and headed for the door of City Hall. Green took a deep breath and then followed after him.

"Mayor Carrington! Do you wish to comment on Blythe's very own vigilante, The Sting?"

Carrington stopped in his tracks and turned around in disbelief. "What?"

"The Sting. That's what witnesses said she called herself while stopping last night's bank robbery." Green held out a digital recorder. "Their description matches the women seen running from the exploding meth lab the night before."

"And you think we have a vigilante?" Carrington began to laugh. "Are you that desperate to get noticed that you want to take two completely unrelated events and sensationalize them?"

"Well, the witnesses…." Green started nervously.

"Are unreliable." Carrington interrupted. "And there is no evidence that the trailer explosion earlier this week was anything more than an accident. Nor any evidence of illegal activity."

"What about the photos?"

"You mean the ones taken by Peter Johnson?" Carrington softened his voice a bit. "They're probably doctored so he could sell them to the Times. You know he used to do special effects in Hollywood, right? I already talked to the editor over there and he's thinking of printing a retraction."

Green shifted his feet a bit. "What about the robbery?"

"A misguided good Samaritan jumped in and tried to help. Luckily no one got hurt." Carrington put his hand on Green's shoulder. "Whoever it was, probably saw the paper that morning and was emboldened to action and could have gotten themselves killed. Running more stories about a fictional vigilante might make someone else decide to try it, maybe with fatal results. Do you really want that on your conscience?"

Green lowered his head a bit. "No. I wouldn't want that to happen."

Carrington gave his best reassuring smile. "I know your heart is in the right place. You want this town to have its own voice again. That's a big responsibility and you have to choose what your write wisely. Keep doing what you're doing, build up your site through legitimate news and information. Stay away from the wild speculation."

"You're right." Green nodded his head. "I'm sorry."

"Call Audrey next week and you can come in and I'll give you an exclusive about our plans for the upcoming renovation of City Hall. That should get you some new viewers. Now, I have a meeting to get to."

"Thank you!" the reporter called after the Mayor.

Carrington walked into his office to find Audrey leaning over her desk, writing a note. He stopped and admired the view for a moment. Audrey stood and turned around. Seeing her boss staring put a big smile on her face.

"Good morning, Mr. Mayor."

His eyes took in his young, beautiful assistant who was wearing what appeared to be a new, red satin dress that clung to her like shrink wrap.

Hiring her as his assistant was the best thing he'd ever done, even if his 56-year old body was having a hard time keeping up. He'd sent her shopping that morning just so he could get another hour or two of sleep.

"New dress?"

She posed for him, showing it off in its best light. "Yes. You have exquisite taste as always."

"Mark the receipt as 'Health & Wellness' and put it in with the rest of the city business." He gestured towards his office. "They here?"

"Yes." She sat down behind her desk. "I'll make sure you're not disturbed."

He nodded his thanks, stared at her ample cleavage for a moment, then opened the door to his office. Inside there were two men waiting. Pacing back and forth along the window was Detective Wade Furlong, whose usual 'resting angry face' seemed to be amplified a bit. His well-worn suit looked to be about ready for the dry cleaners again and his hair hadn't seen a brush in at least a week. The other man in the room was the polar opposite. Tony 'Spanky' Spinello leaned back in a chair like he was about to fall asleep. He wore a well-tailored three-piece suit that included a pocket watch and chain. His hair was heavily slicked back and he had a toothpick hanging from his lip. He stood out in Blythe like a lobster in the desert. You just stared at him wondering how the hell he got there.

Carrington went and placed his satchel on the side table before taking a seat at his desk. Spanky opened his eyes, nodded at the mayor, then lowered them down to about half-mast. Wade stopped in mid stride, spun around and practically jumped into the open chair.

"About time, Rock," Wade barked out. "We've got to get a handle on this shit, now."

"Hold up, Wade." Carrington turned his computer on. "I just walked in the door. Let me get this thing booted up or we're going to miss his call."

Wade jerked his head to the side, looking out the window again and tapping his foot to a speed metal rhythm.

Spanky sighed and leaned his head back. "You really need to cut out those energy drinks."

"What?" Wade snapped. "I've only had two this morning. It's this fucking vigilante. You know that punk, Green, plans on doing a story about her?"

The Mayor carefully typed in his password, 'Audrey382436'. "No, he's not. I already took care of that on the way in here. That's why I'm late. And even if he had, no one reads his blog."

"He was talking about how he was sure the report would go viral," Wade interjected. "That CNN might pick it up."

"Stop worrying about Green." Wade started opening up programs, his email first and then Skype. "What's going on with Jimmy and Chad?"

Wade took a deep breath and seemed to relax a bit. "They're sitting in a holding cell at the station."

"Where a couple of my boys will pick them up in a few minutes and make sure they're no longer an issue." Spanky rolled the toothpick from one side of his mouth to the other. "A shame. Chad was a decent cook."

"They're both as dumb as a box of shit." Carrington shook his head. "And there are always more desperate people waiting to make a fast buck."

Wade smiled at that for a moment before remembering what he had been worked up about. "What are we going to do about this chick in the mask?"

Before Carrington could respond, the electronic jingle sounded that told him his call was coming in. He guided the mouse over to hit accept and the familiar white 'X' against the black background appeared. He grabbed the Bluetooth webcam off the top of his monitor and moved it over to the side table where their fourth guest would be able to see them all.

An electronically modified voice sounded out of the speakers. "You gentleman have had an interesting few days."

Wade jumped in. "We were just talking about the vigilante and how we can catch—"

"Do nothing," the distorted voice commanded.

"What?" Wade jumped to his feet. "That lab was making us good money. She has to be stopped."

"That lab was something I specifically told you was a bad idea," the computer replied. "Putting it in the trailer park was bound to draw attention, which it did. Now it's gone as I assume are the people who were associated with it."

"Happening as we speak," Spanky said.

"I assume you're not going to kill them, are you, Mr. Spinello?"

"Just gonna put the fear of God into them then ship 'em off to my cousin in Jersey." The toothpick rolled again. "He'll keep them off the radar."

"Why don't we just kill them?" Wade asked. "We're in the fucking desert, we could dump a body practically anywhere."

"On the off chance, however unlikely, a body is found, then suddenly there is a lot more attention on us." Carrington glared at Wade.

"Mr. Carrington is correct." After a pause, the unseen caller added, "Some drug deals and a few robberies people will overlook, Detective Furlong, but when bodies start turning up, the people suddenly want answers. A city of quiet, depressed citizens focused on their own pitiful lives is exactly what we need to make money. Let's not destroy that with senseless killing or going on a crusade against a vigilante."

"And what about the people already asking questions?" Carrington asked.

"Deny her existence and change the subject," the speaker said. "People will lose interest quickly when their next bill shows up that they can't pay. There is no vigilante, but I believe you already have a handle on that, don't you, Mayor Carrington?"

"Yes." Carrington sat up straight in his chair. "I already killed the story. We can come up with something for the folks to talk about. Perhaps we can sponsor a pub crawl. People seem to love those and it's good for businesses."

Spanky sat up for the first time and looked into the webcam. "That's all well and good, but I've got a client base that is going to want their drugs and now we're down a lab. You were against it being in the trailer park— fine. Where should the replacement lab go? Because there will be a new lab up and running by the end of the day, make no mistake about that."

"Seriously? Every other lot in the city is vacant. Just don't put it near where people live." Exasperation could almost be heard through the distortion and then a sigh. "Put it out by the auto recycling center. Nobody goes that far south."

"All right." Spinello leaned back into his sleepy look.

"Now, back to the original reason for the meeting," the voice said, regaining its authority. "We should hear from Sacramento soon. Once we know the dates of the grant visit and what they're looking for, we can tailor the presentation accordingly. My insider is telling me that we are one of six cities being considered for the grant."

"Do we know who the other cities are?" the mayor asked.

"Not yet. But you could probably look up the economically poorest cities of California and have a good idea." The distorted voice snickered. "We'll just have to make sure that Blythe is the most desperate of all. Luckily we're starting off with a good foundation of misery."

The mayor smiled, thinking about the grant money. "Is there anything we should do now?"

There was a pause on the line before the voice responded. "Yes. Cut police patrols down about ten percent in the outlying areas. A few extra break-ins will add to the crime rate. And cut the afternoon hours at the library. That should irritate the folks who use it as child care or a computer center."

"Nobody reads anymore anyways." Spinello snorted.

"We'll talk again in a week," the voice said. "And, Detective Furlong, I am very serious. Do nothing about the masked woman. Let it go."

The sound of the call disconnecting played out through the speakers. The three men sat quietly for a moment before Spanky rose to his feet. He made a move to tip a hat that he wasn't wearing and then made his way out of the office, closing the door behind him.

Wade slid forward in his chair. "I think the vigilante lives in the trailer park."

"What?" Carrington shook his head. "You're supposed to leave this alone."

"Come on, Rock!" The detective slapped his hand on the desk between them. "This is our town! We might be listening to that guy because of the money, but he's not our boss. And that girl is messing with our town. We can't let that go unchecked."

"Yes, we can. We absolutely can." The mayor got up from his seat to retrieve the webcam. "We don't even know that it's the same girl."

"Actually, we do." Wade pulled some folded papers out of his back pocket, spread them out and put them on the desk. "I got the footage from the bank and compared it to the photos from the trailer park. It's the same girl."

Carrington glanced down at the two images. The first was the Hollywood looking explosion shot from the paper. The second was the masked woman in the bank talking to Chad. She wasn't wearing the skin-tight black suit in the second shot, but the mask, chest piece and sticks were the same. Even the messy blond hair matched. But that didn't matter. He scooped up the pictures, folded them back together and handed them to Wade just as the detective was starting to stand.

"It doesn't matter. I doubt she'll be stupid enough to do anything else. And as long as we don't do anything stupid, it should all just blow over." He guided Wade towards the door. "Go back to your office, relax and don't do anything stupid."

Wade didn't look happy at all. He took a deep breath then slowly let it out through his nostrils, making a low, whistling sound. He then tucked the papers back into his pocket and left.

Carrington watched him go, and smiled at Audrey before returning to his office. He walked over to the window and gazed out at his city. He hoped they were right, that the woman was nothing more than a coincidence and would fade away with the next news cycle. He assured himself with the knowledge that no one in their right mind would risk their life for Blythe.

CHAPTER FIVE

The next week or so wasn't very good for Erin. Giving in to her anger sent her into a depression where just getting off the couch was more effort than she wanted to exert. Robert was good about it, let her be for a couple days. It wasn't like she had anywhere she was supposed to be. She slept and drank and watched old episodes of cop shows she'd seen a hundred times before. It didn't matter if they were New York cops, L.A. cops or Navy cops, the stories were all the same. A crime was committed, the police got involved and by the end of the hour the bad guy went to jail as neat as you please. After she screamed for ten minutes about how life didn't work that way, Robert came out with a fresh beer and switched the channel to cooking shows and things calmed down again.

Erin wasn't sure how many days had pass. Two, five, maybe a week, but when the smell from the trash got too much, she finally got up to take it out. She opened the lid to find that the bin was empty. A glance around the kitchen showed nothing that could cause the smell, but it was still there. She opened the fridge and saw no rotting leftovers or past date milk. If anything, the fridge was almost empty. There wasn't even any beer left. That was going to be a problem. She swung the door shut, causing a mild breeze to push against her and she found the source of the smell. She hadn't showered in far too long.

She formed a simple plan in her mind. Take a shower, get dressed and then walk to the market to buy more beer. Ten minutes under the water. Her short blond hair was quick to wash and she could just let it dry on the walk. But the idea of doing anything before she had a beer just wasn't sitting well with her. She felt tense and the fact that there wasn't a beer to help her mellow out was making her even more tense. The plan changed in her mind. She'd go get the beer—half the people in the store smelled worse than she did anyway—then come back and shower. That seemed like a much better plan to her.

She grabbed her jeans off the couch and slid them on. They needed to be washed, but were good enough for the walk. She pulled a clean t-shirt from the pile of clothes behind the couch and then put on her sneakers. A check of her pocket found a twenty, two fives and a few singles, enough to get what she wanted. Robert was out somewhere, so she grabbed her keys and locked the trailer behind her.

Counting the distance from the trailer to the front gate, the walk to the store was maybe a mile, give or take. She'd be there and back in under an hour. As she walked, her muscles felt sore. She wasn't sure if was still from the explosion and fight or from being a coach potato for too long. She could feel everything was tight, so she lengthened her stride to try and burn through the aches. A few long strides turned into a jog, and she felt her body protest a little. She didn't like that, so she pushed a little harder, moving up to a run. The muscles in her chest started to twinge and her shoulders began to ache. She pushed harder, moving closer to a sprint. She lowered her head, focusing on the ground beneath her. She felt it in her knees every time one of her feet would slam against the pavement. She kept pushing, trying to go faster. She closed her eyes and focused on the way her lungs were starting to burn. She had to keep going. That was the only thought in her mind at that moment. Keep going. Keep running.

Erin wasn't sure what it was she tripped over. She just felt the toe of her right foot slam against something solid, her body continued to move forward but her leg stayed behind. Her eyes sprung open in time to see the asphalt hurtling towards her. She got her hands up to brace against the impact. She hit hard and felt the skin on her palms tear against the hard ground. Her left shoulder hit next and she could feel the momentum of her body carrying her legs up over her chest. Her knees hit hard and her shoulders came up off the ground. She flipped over two full times before finally coming to rest with her back flat on the ground. She gazed up into the blue sky and strung out a series of curse words like she had never used before.

She laid there in the road for a minute, just taking in deep breaths. Her lungs still ached and she knew she should get out of the road, but she didn't care. She watched as a few clouds passed over head. One looked like a turtle. She liked turtles. She laid there for a few minutes, watching the turtle make its way across the sky and coming to the conclusion that she had to be like that turtle. She needed to suck it up and keep moving forward. One step at a time, moving forward towards a better life. Then she remembered that it was just a cloud and she needed to get out of the fucking street. Or at least that what the lady yelled from the passing car.

Erin sat up and looked around. She had run past the store. That made her laugh a bit. She got to her feet, dusted herself off and started walking back the other way. Her body ached even more than it did when she started, and now her hands and shoulder were pretty scraped up. But she felt a bit better too. She would follow that turtle or cloud and move forward. After she picked up her beer, of course.

With a renewed sense of purpose, Erin got up the next day and cleaned the trailer. She dragged her clothes to the laundromat and cooked the pork chops she found in the freezer for dinner. Robert smiled and ate, but remained skeptical as this wasn't the first renewed sense of purpose Erin had found in the last six months. Truth be told, it was the fourth. It always started with a burst of energy, frantic cleaning and then a determined woman would head out to find a job, only to return home by the end of the day defeated and depressed again.

The next morning Erin put on a pair of dark blue slacks, a white blouse with light blue pipping on the cuffs and collar and a pair of blue pumps. This was her job hunting outfit. Though it was zero for fourteen so far since she bought it. A scan of the Blythe Bulletin's help wanted section showed five listings. Auto mechanic and accountant weren't even worth looking at. Officemart, Louie Louie's and a receptionist position were worth a shot. She had no experience as a receptionist and couldn't type to save her life, but she was feeling optimistic and figured she could at least try. And it was on the way to the other two places.

Robert dropped her off at the place looking for a receptionist, a dentist office. But a sign on the front door told her that the position had already been filled. Knowing it was the biggest long shot, Erin kept her positive attitude and walked the few blocks west to the Officemart. They were just taking applications as the woman who did the interviews wouldn't be back in the area until the following Monday. Seven other people were either filling out an application when she got there or showed up while she was writing. It made sense as they were one of the better paying retail stores in the area.

She hopped on the bus to take her to her final stop. Louie Louie's was a pub style restaurant with a retro '60s theme. The waitresses wore dresses with super shot skirts and low-cut tops. It was the last type of place Erin would want to work. She thought it was demeaning and sexist. But she knew she could fend off any unwanted advances and there weren't many other options. Her dad used to tell her it was easier to get a job when you have a job. She'd convinced herself she could put up with it in the short term to get her life moving again.

She filled out another application, but this time the manager was on hand and could interview here immediately.

"Please, have a seat." The aging bald man with the clip-on tie gestured to an open chair at the last table in the corner. "My name is Jeff."

She took a seat and then extended her hand. "I'm Erin Cooper."

"Nice to meet you, Erin." He shook her hand, then glanced over the resume. "Oh, you're a vet. Thank you for your service."

She nodded, but said nothing as he kept reading.

"No waitressing experience?" He looked up as he asked. "No real work history at all?"

"No. I went into the service shortly after high school," she explained. "Just now getting out into the civilian world."

"Don't worry. The biggest part of the job is dealing with the pressure of angry and impatient customers. I'm sure that will be nothing compare to the military." He laughed and gave a reassuring smile. "We can train you for the rest. It's how you interact with people that matters the most."

From the far-right hand side of the table he pulled out a dessert menu from a metal rack that also held sugar, condiments and seasonings. He handed it over to Erin.

"A lot of our money comes in suggestive sales. People come in looking for dinner, but we want to sell them an appetizer and dessert as well. As a waitress it would be your job to help guide your customers to making additional choices." He sat up straight in his chair. "Let's pretend I've just finished up my lunch of a Country Western Salad and Diet Coke and I may be ready to leave. Try to talk me into a dessert."

Erin glanced at the list, scanning through the options. "Seeing as you had a salad and a diet soda, it's likely you're watching either your calories or your sugar intake, so I'd choose what might sound like the healthy choice. That appears to be the Crustless Apple Pie."

Erin stopped a moment and read the description. Jeff was waiting for her to sell him on it, but the silence drug on for a moment.

"Is something wrong?" Jeff asked.

"How can an apple pie be crustless?" She kept looking at the description. "Pie, by definition, has a crust."

"It's our new carb-friendly option." Jeff leaned over and pointed at the image on the menu. "Its apples, cut into slices, basted with butter then baked. We then sprinkle a bit of oats and sugar on top and bake again."

"How does that make it anything close to pie?" Erin lowered the menu and looked at Jeff. "That's more of an apple crisp. A pie has a crust. No crust, then it's not a pie."

"People who are trying to cut carbs still want to have dessert," Jeff tried to explain. "We're just giving them the option."

"No. You're lying to them to sell a product." Erin looked at the list again. "Here you have chocolate cream pie. If you took the crust away, it doesn't make it crustless chocolate cream pie, it makes it chocolate pudding, or maybe chocolate mousse. Do you think it helps your customers to think they're getting pie when they're not?"

Jeff got up from the table. "I'm sorry, Erin, but I don't think you're the right fit for Louie Louie's."

Erin leapt to her feet. "Why? Because I won't shill out the corporate bullshit?"

Jeff took a few steps back and put his hands up defensively. "Yes. That's exactly why."

She looked at Jeff and then sighed. She turned and made her way for the door. She was so disappointed in herself, she didn't notice the guy at the bar getting up to follow her out.

"Ma'am! Wait!"

Erin didn't hear the voice the first two times. But she finally turned around when he yelled out, "Stop!"

"What?" Erin took a few steps back towards the man who had been trying to get her attention.

He was slender and stood maybe five-eight or five-nine. He had sandy-blond hair that needed a trim and a somewhat patchy goatee. He wore a pair of blue framed glasses, new looking jeans, a dress shirt with no tie and the sleeves rolled up and a pair of tan hiking boots that may have never seen the dirt, even in the desert. If she had to guess, she'd say he was in his early twenties and that might be being generous.

"I couldn't help but overhearing your conversation with the manager in there." He reached out his hand. "My name is Bernie Greene and I'm with the Blythe Bulletin."

"And?" Erin stared at him, leaving his hand dangling in the air.

"And, I would like to offer you a job."

Erin took a step to the side and leaned up against a Ford Explorer that was parked in the handicapped space. She folded her arms, continuing to stare at Bernie.

"What kind of job?" She locked eyes with him. "And why me?"

Bernie shifted a little. "I currently am the only employee at the bulletin, and on most days, that's fine. Not a lot happening in Blythe. But there seems to be this feeling like something's coming. I don't know if it's just the vigilante and the meth lab explosion, but I think I'm going to need some help soon."

She gestured for him to keep going. "And the second part?"

"I've got a problem dealing with authority." His face turned a little red. "I'm good at doing research and putting pieces together, but I turn into a marshmallow around authority figures. I tried to get a quote out of the mayor this morning about the Sting and he sent me away like I'd just been caught stealing from the cookie jar. I watched you stand up for something you believed in against someone you needed something from. And you stood your ground."

"Because I'm a moron." She shook her head. "I cost myself a job because I couldn't just smile and toe the line."

"And that is exactly what the Bulletin needs." He smiled at her. "You need a job. I need some help. Come try it out for a few months. Either you'll like it or you'll be getting a paycheck while you look for something better later."

"You know absolutely nothing about me." Erin took a step towards Bernie. "How do you know you can trust me?"

"I don't. But you served your country and you know that you can't have a pie without a crust. That seems like a good enough place to start."

He held out his hand again. This time, Erin shook it.

CHAPTER SIX

Erin took the bus back to the trailer park and was walking towards Robert's trailer when she noticed someone sitting on the small bench by the front door. Peter Johnson was leant back against the trailer with his eyes closed. As she got close, she saw that his chest was rising and falling in a slow, smooth rhythm, and she started to hear snoring. The old man had fallen asleep. She stopped a few feet back and said his name, not wanting to startle him. "Mr. Johnson?"

The man snorted once, his head rolled to the right, and then he went right back to snoring.

Erin repeated his name, only louder this time. "Mr. Johnson."

The old man opened his left eye, looked at her, then around, then closed it again. A second later his snoring resumed.

She stared for a moment in disbelief, then spoke loudly. "Mr. Johnson!"

"I'm not deaf, you know," the man said, this time not moving at all. "You could give an old man a heart attack, yelling like that."

Shaking her head, she started up the steps to the door of the trailer. "Rest there as long as you need. I'm going inside."

"I'm not resting, I'm waiting for you."

She stopped and looked back at the man on the bench. "Why?"

"I've got something for you." He opened his eyes. "Back at my trailer."

"Does that line ever work?" She turned to face him. "I don't even know you."

Johnson got up and straightened his shirt tails. "Ancient Chinese saying: you squash a man's petunias and you're bonded for life."

Erin tried to hide her surprise. "That's not a saying. And I haven't been anywhere near your petunias."

He started walking towards his trailer. "If that wasn't your butt sticking up from my flower bed the other night, then they might as well just put me in the ground, because I'm hallucinating."

Erin stood on the top step and though about it. She'd been wearing a mask the night of the meth lab explosion. There should be no way the old man could know it was her. Yet there he was, acting like he was certain. And what did he want? He hadn't told the cops or the newspapers it was her. Was he trying to blackmail her? Was he some kind of pervert? The smart move would be to just deny even knowing what he was talking about and hope he went away. But she'd already proven she didn't go with the smart moves.

She followed Mr. Johnson across the trailer park to his unit in the back. All of his flowers were back in their places and looking fine. No indication she'd ever crashed into them in the first place. She waited as he unlocked three deadbolts and then the door handle. He didn't say a word through any of it, didn't look back to see if she was there. He just opened the door, walked in and left it open for her to follow. She hesitated for just a moment, but curiosity outweighed caution and she stepped inside.

What she saw inside stunned her. A full-body mannequin stood in the corner, wearing what appeared to be some kind of battle / tactical suit. It seemed to be based loosely on the on the paintball gear she'd been wearing before, but it was *much* more impressive. The base color was black, and looked a lot like the Kevlar vests she'd used in the military. Breaking up the black were thicker areas of gold along the outer thighs, abdomen, forearms and biceps. There were also black and gold boots, with guards that came up over the knees, as well as shoulder pads and a belt with pockets for storage.

Mr. Johnson moved over and tapped the suit. "The black area is a Kevlar-based weave that can protect from small caliber handgun and shotgun rounds. It will also help against small explosive projectiles like hand grenades, and should do pretty well in stopping a knife thrust. The gold areas have ceramic plates stitched in, which should provide even more protection. I did them in hopes of drawing your opponent's attention to those spots. It won't stop a high-powered round, but it should afford you a bit more protection than a wet suit and plastic paintball gear."

Erin stepped up and felt the black fabric. "It's thin. The gear we had in the army was bulky."

"And way out of date." Johnson started opening a box as he talked. "The gear the military uses is based on technology from the 90s, and mass produced. I know some folks working with the absolute newest materials. I called in a few favors."

She stared at the outfit, then forcefully reminded herself of the current situation. "This is impressive and all. But why are you showing me? And what is this for?"

He ignored her questions and pulled the helmet from out of the box. It was similar to the mask she had borrowed from Robert, but also seemed sturdier. The face's mouth and nose portion seemed a bit thicker, but the visor still had the gold, reflective lenses.

"I kept the basic design of the mask you used, but I coated the lens with graphene and worked a filtration system into the ventilation that can keep out toxins and smoke." He turned it around to show the closure. "The latch is biometrically triggered to finger prints. Once we put yours into the mask, only you can take it off. Even if you get knocked out, the mask will stay in place."

He handed her the mask and then pulled out another box from the corner. The mask looked perfect. She really wanted to try it on, but if she did, she'd be admitting that she was the person who attacked the meth lab.

He stopped and glanced up at her. "I get that you are trying to keep who you are a secret. I understand. And I wouldn't have said a word, but the gear you were wearing was not going to help you at all. And I couldn't in good conscience allow you to roam the streets in paintball gear when I could do something about it."

She looked into the older man's eyes and realized that she was fighting a losing battle. "I don't know what you think, but that was just a one-time – okay, two-time thing. I'm not a vigilante and I won't be suiting up again."

Mr. Johnson turned and leaned back against the counter, shaking his head a bit. "That's a shame. The people of this city are going to be very disappointed. For the first time in a very long time, they were starting to feel hope gain."

"Hope?" Erin was genuinely surprised. "At what? How I almost got everyone in the park killed, or how I almost got people shot in the bank? I recklessly charged into two separate situations without any thought about the ramifications. The only hope this town should have is hope that I move on soon."

"You tried to make a difference, when no one else has." He grabbed a copy of the paper with her on the cover, and showed it to her. "What everyone in the city saw in this picture was a hero, standing up for them when the cops and politicians refused to. These people have been shit on by everyone and left to suffer in the middle of nowhere. People don't live in Blythe. They die here. But you gave them just an ounce of hope that maybe somebody out there actually gives a damn for them."

She stared silently at the mask for a moment. Was she the threat to everyone around her that Robert suggested, or a symbol of hope like Mr. Johnson talked about? And how had that even become the question? All she'd wanted to do was to come home and start living her life.

"I get it. This wasn't what you were trying to do." He turned back to the suit. "Can you do me a favor at least. Try it on. I've never worked with graphene before, and I'd like to see how it moves. Plus, we'll see if I can still eyeball somebody's measurements."

She nodded in agreement, and Mr. Johnson stepped out of the room so she could change. She took the suit off the mannequin first, amazed at how light it felt. She could tell it was going to be tight, so she stripped down to her bra and underwear before realizing where she was.

"You're not peeking, are you?" She called out.

"Of course I am," he yelled back. "I'm seventy-two years old, and don't get many pretty women coming by the trailer anymore."

She thought about it for a moment, shrugged and pulled on the skin-tight body suit. It went on a bit easier than her wetsuit had, and the ceramic and graphene plates were molded to her curves. The old man's measurements were seriously impressive. She had everything on except the helmet and gloves when Johnson returned.

"Let's get you coded to the lock." He picked up the helmet and used his middle finger to open the latch, then held it out to her. "Put your middle finger over that square. You're going to feel a tiny pin prick. It will then code to both your finger print and DNA."

"It's going to stick my finger each time I take the helmet off?" she asked.

"No. It will go by your finger print first. But if for some reason that finger isn't available, it will check DNA as a backup."

She put the helmet on and locked it into place. It fit snugly, and the lenses gave great visibility. Finally, she slid the gloves on, and took a look in the full-length mirror in the corner. There were hint elements of the suit she'd thrown together to take out the meth lab, but this was so much better. It didn't feel like any of the gear she'd worn in the Army. It wasn't bulky or heavy at all.

"You say…" Erin stopped, stunned by the sound of her own voice. "What the fuck?"

Johnson was opening the other box and laughed. "Forgot to warn you about the voice changer built into the mask. Sorry about that."

She sounded like a pack a day smoker using a Vox, giving her voice a deep, raspy sound with an almost melodic flow. She sounded like a female Louie Armstrong. She fought the urge to singe, "What a Wonderful World."

"I noticed you carrying a pair of escrima sticks." He pulled a pair of black sticks out of the box. "I had these made. They're a titanium-aluminum mix, coated in two layers of graphene. Should be light enough to use, sturdy enough to break bones, and strong enough to knock a bullet out of the air if you want to go full ninja."

She took the sticks and swung them a few times. "Nice. Really good balance. You've mentioned graphene a few times. What the hell is it?"

"The short answer, it's a layer of carbon atoms arranged in a hexagonal pattern." The old man put one hand over the other. "Recently scientists figured out that if they put two layers together, that the stuff reacts to pressure by turning into an almost diamond-hard substance. Makes it somewhat bullet resistant. But it only works with two layers. The effect is not as profound with three or more. So, two is as sturdy as it gets. It also conducts electricity well, disperses heat, and dissipates momentum."

"And how did you get your hands on it?" she asked.

"I spent most of my life designing suits and tech for the film industry." He started digging into the box again. "But I did some side work occasionally for a couple weapons manufacturers and had a few friends in high places."

He pulled a black case out of the box and opened it up. Erin moved closer and saw what appeared to be a slightly oversized semi-automatic pistol, similar in design to the Beretta 96 A1, but bigger. It had a laser sight on the rail below the barrel and an oversized magazine that stuck out a good four inches below the handle.

"What is that?"

Johnson checked to make sure there wasn't a round chambered and then handed the gun over. "It's a custom-made .40 caliber pistol with 25-round magazines, and it can fire in single shot or three-round bursts. We call it the Wishmaster. You want someone dead, it will grant your wish."

Erin took the gun, and checked the action. She popped out the magazine, saw the rounds, then slapped it back in and chambered the first bullet. Unlike everything else here, the gun had some heft to it. Which she'd need, with recoil from three-round bursts. Even with its oversized grip, it felt good in her hand. She hadn't held a gun since leaving the service. She spun it around once on her index finger then jammed it into her hip holster. It fit perfectly, just like everything else that Johnson had presented her.

"I'll give you credit, you've made one bad-ass vigilante suit." She slid the sticks into their sheaths on her back. "If I was going to go out and prowl the night looking for evil-doers, this is *definitely* the suit I'd want. But I'm afraid you wasted your time. I'm nobody's hero."

The first pop could've been a car backfiring. At two, it still might've been fireworks. By the third though, she knew that they were getting closer. By the fourth, she'd pushed Mr. Johnson to the ground and was turning towards the door. The fifth, sixth and seventh shots tore through the metal walls of the trailer. One bullet bounced off her right shoulder while the second hit her square in the gut. The third ripped through the mannequin and continued through to shatter a window on its way out.

The popping sounds continued, but they seemed to be moving further away again. She looked down at her stomach. No blood. On the floor at her feet were two smashed bullets, .223's if she had to guess. She quickly moved to Johnson to check on him.

"I'm fine!" He pushed her hands away. "Go after them!"

Erin should've stopped. She should have thought about what had just happened. Why was someone shooting at them? Were they the only targets? Who was shooting? But she could still hear the gunfire. So, instead, she threw open the door, and without a second of reflection, raced out into danger.

CHAPTER SEVEN

Erin leapt down the steps and out into the road that ran through the trailer park. She glanced around quickly, seeing bullet holes in most of the trailers around her. Whoever was doing the shooting, they weren't specifically targeting her or Mr. Johnson. They were just shooting at everything—retaliating for her attack on the meth lab. It was the only thing that made sense. Since they didn't know exactly who'd done it, they'd decided to make everyone pay. People were getting hurt, and she needed to stop it.

A glance to the left showed her a boy standing near a trailer a few up from Johnson's. He looked unhurt, but in shock. He saw Erin in her tactical suit and then pointed further up the road. She heard more shots from the same direction. The bad guys were heading through the back of the park. She hadn't lived there long, but she knew the two-car path that wound through the park from the single front gate, past all of the spaces. Instead of racing off after them, she cut straight across, dashing between two trailers on the opposite side of the road.

She hurdled a small fence that separated a couple of spaces, listening to the sounds of the gun shots. They were getting closer now. She crossed the cul-de-sac, heading towards another pair of back-to-back lots. Instead of going between the trailers this time, she used the bumper of a pickup to leap onto its bedcover, then up onto the cab. From there, it was a short jump onto the roof of the trailer. She raced along the length of the mobile home and put everything she had into the eight-foot vault to the next trailer.

Only the front half of her foot caught the edge, but her momentum carried her forward into a roll. She came up on one knee and saw a chocolate brown Buick LeSabre heading her way. Any doubt that this was the right car was immediately washed away by the guy sitting half out of the passenger window. He was holding an AR-15 and firing off rounds at each trailer as the car moved along.

She pulled out one of the sticks and sprung to her feet, sprinting across the roof. Without a second of hesitation, she dove at the LeSabre's roof as it passed. The gunman froze—a masked woman in black and gold flying towards him must've caught him by surprise. She swung the stick down as hard as she could, hitting his arm. He dropped the rifle. With her other hand, she grabbed him by the shirt. Her feet swung around and flew off the side of the car, but the shirt held. She pulled herself back up solidly onto the roof, ignoring the choking sounds the man was making.

Now gunless, he twisted around and forced his elbow down hard onto her arm, forcing her to let go of his collar. He leaned across and pinned her to the roof, then slammed his other fist down into her face. The mask lessened the blow, but it still hurt like hell. Her eyes immediately watered. The guy raised his fist to strike again.

Erin hooked her arm around his and pulled, swinging her entire body across the roof, with her feet around his midsection. Suddenly all of her weight and momentum was crashing into his back. The two of them tumbled onto the ground. They crashed down on the asphalt, her back taking the brunt of it. She felt the air fly out of her lungs. The car kept going.

Gunless quickly slid off of her and onto his knees. He braced himself, and slammed his fist down into her stomach. She gasped desperately for breath. The guy threw another punch into the center of her chest, hard enough to break bones—had it not been for the suit. It wasn't protecting her completely, but it dispersed enough of the impact to give her a fighting chance.

The guy raised both hands over his head for a knock-out strike. She drove her knee into his unprotected groin as savagely as she could. He let out a high-pitched, wheezy yelp, arms sagging. As his guard dropped, she smashed a knuckle punch into the right side of his throat. He fell over sideways, gagging. She got to her knees, found the escrima stick she'd dropped, and grasped it in her right hand.

"I'd say I'm sorry," she said, raising the stick up, "but that would be a lie."

She struck him across the left temple, knocking him out cold. She stared at him for a moment, then climbed to her feet, staggering back a bit as she tried to catch her breath. The guy was down, but there was something she was forgetting. And that's when it hit her. The LeSabre.

Literally.

The car slammed into the back of her legs. She flew up onto the hood with a loud thud. The breath that she still hadn't really caught whooshed back out of her. The car slammed to a stop, and she was thrown forward. She turned in the air and hit the ground face and shoulder first, then continued on over, landing flat on her back again. Serious pain flooded her, and her body vetoed her desperate orders to move. She heard the car door open, and turned her head enough to see the driver getting out. He looked young.

"Who the fuck are you?" the man said, as he approached.

"Park security." Her filtered voice sounded even weirder than before, as she was short of breath. "You don't have the proper tag to be here."

"You're seriously making jokes? And wearing a costume?" He shook his head. "I'm not sure if that makes you a smart ass or a dumb ass."

"Probably a little of both," she admitted.

"Doesn't matter anyway. We'll just I.D. the corpse." The man pulled his jacket back to pull a gun out of a belt holster and she stared in disbelief. A gold badge was clipped to his belt. Not only was he a cop, but he was dumb enough to wear his badge while shooting up the place.

"Hey, Barney Fife, you probably want to stop before you do something even more stupid."

He just shook his head and aimed his gun at her. "You must've been the life of the party. The party's over."

His 9mm barked once, and Erin felt something slam into her gut. She was wondering if she would ever get to take a normal breath again when a second shot fired. It didn't hit her. Instead it went sailing into the air, the shooter spasming like crazy. He dropped to the ground, to reveal Mr. Johnson holding a stun gun in one hand and an inhaler in the other. He began taking deep puffs off of it.

"Sorry…" he gasped between hits. "I just can't run like I used to."

She forced herself to look down at her stomach, expecting to see blood. Instead she found a smashed bullet pressed against one of the gold plates. There wasn't even a scratch on the suit. The thing was amazing. She rolled onto her side slowly and took a slow, deep breath. After another second or two, she felt confident enough to try and stand. It was a bit shaky, but she successfully got to her feet. She checked on the first guy. He was still out cold. The driver was starting to move. She slammed the heel of her boot into his face, ending that.

She found his keys and walked over to the trunk of the car. She rummaged around and came up with a couple of rags and some duct tape. Then she headed back to the two unconscious shooters.

"Want me to call the cops?" Johnson asked.

Erin flipped open the driver's coat. "These *are* the cops."

Johnson's eyes got huge. "Holy shit. What are you going to do with them?"

He couldn't see it through the mask, but she smiled. "Oh, I have an idea."

She secured both men and sat them in the back seat of the car, seat belts on. The rags stuck in their mouth would keep them from talking while she drove. She tossed the remaining duct tape into the trunk and was about to close it when she noticed a blue canvas sports bag. Brand new, it stood out compared to the rest of the junk in the trunk. She zipped it open and found stacks and stacks of cash. It was all small denominations, but there was still a good amount of money there. She took it with her and closed the trunk, tossing the bag on the front passenger seat.

She turned to Johnson. "You own a car or something?"

"Yup."

"Meet me behind the Best Western in about thirty minutes." She slid inside the car. "And bring my clothes from your trailer."

He nodded as she turned over the engine and pulled away. It was a gamble. She was counting on two different people she'd just met—not something she'd ever normally do. It seemed like her only option, though. As she drove out of the park, an ambulance went flying by. She hoped no one was seriously hurt.

The sun was down by the time she pulled into the parking lot outside the two-story office building that contained the Blythe Bulletin. It was on the first floor, far left side, and the light was still on through the window. She parked the car and got out. Her passengers were struggling against their restraints, but didn't seem to be going anywhere. She stepped over a small bush and tapped on the window. After a second, a familiar face peeked through the blinds and then his eyes went wide. Erin waited for a second. Bernie just starred at her. She gestured for him to come outside. He slowly nodded and let the blinds go.

A minute later, the young reporter burst out of the front door carrying an armful of technology including a camera, a voice recorder and a tablet. Erin was leaning against the LeSabre's fender.

"Oh my god," Bernie shouted, "you're the Sting!"

"Bring it down a notch, I'm right here," she replied.

"What are you doing here?" He looked around the parking lot in confusion.

"I'm bringing you tomorrow's headline." She gestured to the two guys in the back of the car. "These assholes just shot up the trailer park as retaliation for me taking down the meth lab."

He held up his camera. "May I?"

"By all means." Erin stepped out of the shot.

Bernie took a few pictures of the guys in the car, the car itself, and the AR-15 that was sitting between them. "Is that loaded?"

"No. I took the magazine out and tossed it in the trunk." She reached in and grabbed the sports bag. "Safety first."

"I appreciate you bringing them here, but why not take them to the cops?"

She pointed at the driver. "Because that one is a cop. If I dropped them off at the station, I'd be arrested, and I'm guessing these boys would go free."

"Son of a—" Bernie took a deep breath. "What am I supposed to do with them?"

That was an excellent question. "I'd say write up a quick version of the story and post it immediately, *then* call the cops. Once the information is out there, you should be fine."

He held his camera up again. "A picture of you would help sell the story."

She paused. It felt like the point of no return. *Oh well.* She put the bag down onto the hood and struck the most heroic pose she could. The camera clicked a couple of times.

The die was cast.

"That suit is really impressive," Bernie said. "Something a real, full-time vigilante might wear. Is that what you are?"

"I don't know what I am yet," she admitted. "I didn't wake up one day and decide I wanted to fight crime like some comic book character. I just got tired of seeing people suffer, and I wanted to help. It kind of got out-of-hand."

Bernie put his camera down. "I don't know you or have any idea of what you are risking by putting on that mask. I don't know what this is doing to you. I do know what it's doing to the people who live in this city, though. They're talking about you. They're excited that someone cares. Even if you never suit up again, you've given the people of Blythe a reminder that there is still justice in this world. You've given them hope. They believe in the Sting."

She shook her head. "I wasn't serious about the name when I said it in the bank. I was just trying to distract the guy."

"You want me to use a different one?"

Erin thought for a moment, but nothing better came to mind. All the good names were taken by movies and television. 'The Sting' was a Paul Newman movie, but at least it wasn't about a superhero. "No. Just leave it. It's not the worst name ever."

She walked over to the car and opened the back door. Then she pulled out one of her sticks and poked the first guy in the leg with it, to get his attention.

"If you were just listening, you may have picked up that I'm conflicted about being a dedicated, full-time vigilante." She whacked the driver's leg, and he groaned through his gag. "What I *am* dedicated to is making your lives an absolute hell. If I find out that you escape jail and end up back out, I promise that I will find you and beat the shit out of you on a regular basis until you pull your worthless asses into a cell and lock the door behind you. Am I clear?"

The two men nodded emphatically. She smacked them both in their stomachs, one last bit of payback for all their punches and bullets. Then she closed the door, grabbed the sports bag, and started to walk away.

Bernie seemed surprised. "You're walking?"

She looked back over her shoulder. "Uber drivers don't like passengers in masks. Something about making them nervous. Now get writing. You have a story to post."

Jogging around the backside of the building, she saw the lit-up sign for Best Western. A quick scan around didn't show anyone watching. Her body ached, and it still hurt a bit to breathe. All she wanted to do was get home, take a long, hot shower, and sleep for a month.

CHAPTER EIGHT

Erin was surprised to find that Mr. Johnson hadn't shown. Instead, she saw Robert's truck idling with the lights off. She hesitated for a second, unsure. He rolled the window down and waved her over, so she sprinted across the parking lot and climbed in the passenger side. Her clothes sat, neatly stacked, on the seat between them. She pulled off her glove and released the lock on her mask, then removed it and placed it on the floorboard between her feet.

"What are you doing here?" She took off her other glove.

Robert put the truck into drive and left the parking lot. "I went over to see what all the noise was, and found Mr. Johnson heading to his car, carrying your clothes. Thought I'd stop and find out what the hell was going on. He told me about the shooting and what you were doing. I offered to pick you up instead. He wasn't breathing very well."

"I appreciate that."

"No problem." Robert turned away from the trailer park. "By the way, what the hell are you wearing?"

She stopped tugging on her boot and looked at it. "Oh yeah. This is something Johnson made up. I guess he used to design costumes for the movies. He thought I was trying to do this full-time and needed an upgrade."

"That's not a costume." He reached over and touched her arm, feeling the material. "That's some serious body armor. Much better than the stuff you and I had in Afghanistan."

She slid out of the suit, leaving her in just her bra and underwear. Robert turned his head away, which made her smile. She slipped on her jeans and top, and then realized that they were getting on the freeway, heading west.

"Where are we going?"

He didn't answer, just pulled the truck onto the 10, eyes on the road.

Erin studied him. He had that determined look on his face that meant he wouldn't say another word, at least not until he was ready to. She glanced around to see if she could figure it out.

Oh.

Her duffle bag was in the back of the truck. She'd never unpacked it, trying to stay as unobtrusive as she could in his trailer. Now she wouldn't need to. Everything she had that wasn't in her father's storage was in that bag.

Well over thirty minutes went by in silence. They'd already passed the aptly named Desert Center. She figured she could last maybe another five minutes. Patience had never been her strong point. He wouldn't be rushed, but it didn't stop her wanting to slap him until he spoke.

To her surprise, she made it ten.   "Will you say something!"

He didn't react, at first. Just kept his eyes on the road. After a minute or two, he sighed, long and deep. He wasn't happy about what he was doing, but he was close to telling her what it was. Another minute went by before he finally spoke.

"I knew something bad was going to happen before we headed out that night." His voice cracked as he spoke. "We were assured the intel was solid. A simple smash and grab on a low-level target. In and out without a single shot fired. But I knew it was bullshit. That's why I asked the Major to put you on the roof."

Erin turned to stare at him. "You did *what?*"

"I told him you were the best shot in the unit, which was true." He finally glanced at her. "But my gut was telling me that it was going to go south, and I didn't want you anywhere near it."

"Why?" She could feel her pulse thumping in her temples. "Was it because you thought I couldn't do my job, or because I'm a mere woman?"

"Neither, and it wasn't because I had feelings for you either." He turned away again, back to the road. "It was because I saw something in you—that you could do great things, and shouldn't die in the sand in a terrorist-run country. But it didn't matter. Things went to hell on a colossal scale and instead of staying on the roof, you came charging in like John-fucking-Wayne to save the day."

"So? What's your point?"

"I lost my leg over there, but you lost more than that. You're broken now. I hoped giving you a place to stay would help you get back on your path. But even your visits to Hertzberg don't seem to be helping. You're dressing up as a comic book character, and he thinks it's a good idea. You saved my life. I wanted to help you get yours back, but I only made it worse. You went after that meth lab because of me, and now you're going up against guys with guns. You need to be away from me."

She felt the pressure building up inside of her. "How very patronizing. That's not your decision to make. You had no right to put me on the sidelines in Afghanistan any more than you do now. Yes, you pointed out the meth lab, but I'm the one who decided to do something about it. I'm the one who decided to go into the bank. And if I get myself killed because I want to try and help people, none of that is on you. I'm not your responsibility." She took a deep breath, and tried to calm herself a little.

"You're damn right you're not." He growled back at her. "So I'm taking you to Indio. Hertzberg has an office where he takes appointments once a week, and there's five hundred dollars in your pants pocket. You can hop a bus or stay there. It's a big enough city you can try to find work there."

"I already have a God damn real, paying job. In Blythe. Working for the paper."

He didn't look at her. "You can decide what you do next. But I'm done."

She fought down a growl. "So the way *you* see it—and correct me if I'm wrong—I saved your life, which broke me, then you made it worse and what, drove me insane or something, so you're dumping me out on the streets to wallow in my insanity with like a week of cash before I go full homeless, in an entirely different city to the one my new job is in. What a *great* way to say thanks, Robert. You're a real hero."

He looked pained, but kept his mouth shut and his eyes glued to the road.

Erin turned to stare pointedly out of the side window. Afghanistan swarmed out of the dark desert to engulf her thoughts.

She'd been surprised to pull cover duty, but you didn't question orders. At least not when it came to missions. She had set up on the roof of a two-story building on the edge of the village, as spec ops had suggested. Her scope gave her a clear view of everything.

Dutch was in the lead, with Hampton and Ramirez close behind. Robert and Simpson were in the rear. It was a small village, maybe a dozen buildings total, mostly one and two-storey. The plan was to slip in from the south, enter the target location as quietly as possible, grab the guy who was their objective, and go. Erin was to make sure no-one tried to follow.

She watched the team move carefully towards their target. None of the residents were stirring, not at three in the morning. Guards might still have been up, but in a quiet spot like that, odds were they'd have nodded off as well. The team were maybe 15 yards from the target when Dutch put his hand on top of his head, signaling her to do a visual sweep before they entered the building.

She quickly scanned through the village, looking for any movement at all—windows, walking paths, corners, anything. The place was completely still. She whispered 'all clear' into her mic, and Dutch motioned the team forward. He stood his ground, gun at the ready. Hampton and Ramirez advanced, setting up on either side of the doorway. Robert and Simpson moved in for the door. Simpson grabbed the handle and pushed. The door opened, but Robert hesitated for two seconds before following Simpson in.

That hesitation saved his life.

The explosion tore Simpson to shreds, killing him instantly. The shrapnel tore through Robert's leg. If he'd been a step further in, he would've been pulverized. The shooting followed immediately from inside the house. Ramirez returned fire while Hampton moved from cover, hooked his hands under Robert's arms, and pulled him back. Hampton took a round to the shoulder, but never wavered for an instant until he had Robert back with Dutch, behind cover.

Erin watched enemy fighters pour out of multiple locations. "You've got a shit ton of uglies coming your way."

"Can we retreat the way we came?" Dutch's voice crackled in her earphone.

She scanned around. "Negative. Maybe a half-dozen coming that way. Let me clear a path."

Erin lined up a shot at the first guy moving on their position from the front of the squad, and put a round through the side of his head. She swung her Barrett rifle around to aim at the ones coming in from behind. They were ducking in and out of cover, and she didn't have time to wait for a clear shot. She squeezed the trigger, and hit a wall about a foot behind the lead fighter. He was dumb enough to look for where the shot had come from, and she fired again, putting a round through his left eye. As he dropped, the others took cover. It bought the team a minute.

She switched back to the other group and sent them to cover too. Moving back and forth, she forced both groups to stop advancing on the squad. But time was running out.

Dutch buzzed in her ear again. "Ramirez is down." His voice ached with fear. "How's that path coming?"

"Doing my best, but they're not cooperating." She fired again. "Four guns to the south. Nine coming in from the north and west."

"Even I can play those odds." Dutch sighed. "I've called in an airstrike. They're five minutes out. We're heading south. In two minutes I want you off that roof and out of the zone. Clear?"

"As root beer." She fired another round at the larger group, forcing them to duck.

She spared a glance for her team. Robert was hopping on his good leg, leaning against Hampton. Dutch was in the lead. They were headed back the way they'd come. She swung her sights towards the group in the way of their retreat and found a tiny target, a three-inch gap in a stack of boxes one of the bad guys was using for cover. She took him in the throat. He staggered forward, grasping his bleeding neck. She didn't have time to finish him.

She turned back to the larger group and saw them advancing, all apart from one guy who was throwing a grenade—at her. Leaving her Barrett behind, she scrambled to her feet and ran. She leapt off the roof towards an adjacent one-story building, hit that roof, and rolled just as the grenade exploded precisely where she'd been. The guy had a hell of an arm. She got back to her feet and kept moving, not wanting to find out if he'd seen her jump and had a second grenade.

Dropping down to the ground, she took an instant to orient, and started running. No way she was leaving without the others. She heard the smaller group open fire. They'd engaged with the team. Three on three. She pulled her Beretta 9mm without slowing down. The layout of the village was fresh in her mind. The southern group would have the squad pinned down, with the larger group advancing on them from behind. It would be over in seconds. She raced around the corner of a building, straight for the remaining members of the southern group.

They weren't expecting an attack from behind. They'd only taken cover from the squad and from her roof. Bad mistake. Her first two quick shots hit one guy in the back. He staggered, and took a third round in the chest. A second gunman began to turn, raising his AK-47. Erin dove forward into a roll, letting the three-shot burst fly over her. She fired off five rounds, knowing her accuracy would be for shit. The first took out the guy's knee, the second smashed up his groin, and the final three tore holes in his chest. As he hit the ground, she saw the third one firing at her.

Rounds grazed her leg and side, then a third one buried itself in her chest. It hurt like hell, and suddenly she was having a hard time raising her arm to fire back.

The gunman's head exploded.

"Move it!" Dutch shouted. He raced over and pulled her to her feet. They began to run. Every step hurt like fire, but bullets were whizzing past them. They reached the outer edge of the village. There was no cover ahead, but no options either. And that was when she had heard the fighters zoom by overhead, and the night had exploded.

She jumped slightly as they came to a halt.

Robert had pulled up at a truck stop on the eastern edge of Indio. There was a motel behind the rest area, but she couldn't see the sign from where they were parked.

She looked him in the eyes. "You're really going to do this?"

"Are you really going to keep running around the streets like some kind of damn superhero?"

She already knew her answer. "Yes."

He simply nodded.

She got out of the truck, pulled her duffle bag out of the back, and crammed the pieces of the suit into it, then slung it up onto her shoulder and looked at her friend. Neither of them said a word. She closed the door and watched as the truck drove away.

CHAPTER NINE

Officer Kent Palmer sat with his back against the wall, waiting for someone to come let him out of the cell. Dwayne lay on the floor, whistling, perfectly at ease. It was the amount of time the man had spent in here, for possession and other offenses, that had led to them becoming friends in the first place. So when Furlong had told him to make an example of the trailer park, Dwayne had been the guy Kent had thought of—the perfect combo of skills, character, and a total lack of credibility in front of a judge.

But here Kent was, inside a cell, all because of that damn bitch. She'd dared to attack him? He was only doing his job. The city would be better off without all the trash in that park anyway. He got to his feet and walked to the bars. *Why the hell am I still in here?*

"Hey!" he yelled. "Where the hell is Furlong?"

There was no reply. No-one came to the door to tell him what was going on. There wasn't even any sound of movement. He'd sat at the desk on the other side of the door thousands of times. You could hear every sound from the cells. He could always hear Dwayne whistling, so whoever was on duty could obviously hear his yelling.

"Where's Furlong?" he shouted again. "Answer me, God damn it!"

"Chill, man."

Kent spun around and looked down at Dwayne, who didn't even have his eyes open. "Why should I chill? We shouldn't be in here."

"But we are." Dwayne opened his eyes and raised himself up onto his elbows. "And in all the times I've been in here, never once did yelling at that door do anyone a lick of good. Just relax. They'll be here when they're here."

"You're a moron." Kent stomped back over to the bench and sat down.

He'd just leaned back against the wall when he heard steps approach the door. There was the sound of keys in the lock, and finally the door swung open. He wanted to leap up and demand to be released, but he decided to take Dwayne's advice and chill. Just wait and see what was going to happen.

Furlong walked through the door, followed by some guy with a toothpick in his mouth. He shut the door behind them, and kept his distance while the detective came up to the bars.

"I'm sorry to keep you waiting." Furlong hunted through his keys. "I had to make some arrangements."

Kent got to his feet. "What kind of arrangements, Wade? You open the door and let me out. It's not difficult."

"You allowed yourself to be caught and delivered to a reporter." The detective unlocked and opened the cell door. "That makes things a bit more complicated."

"How?" Kent reached down and helped Dwayne to his feet. "No-one will take some masked freak bitch seriously, and once we smack the reporter around a bit, he'll stay quiet."

"If only. Green already posted the story, complete with images of you, and called every newspaper and television station in the country to share the story of The Sting's latest bust." Wade shook his head. "That white-haired idiot on CNN was showing your picture to the world just twenty minutes ago. We can't just sweep this under the rug."

Kent stood directly in front of his boss and locked eyes with him. "What's the plan then?"

The toothpick guy stepped forward. "A couple of my boys are going to get you out of town. We'll find you some place to lay low. We get rid of this vigilante problem and a month or two down the line, you come back."

"No way." Kent turned back to Wade. "This was your idea. I'm not taking the heat on this. You fix it, now."

"I'm going to, but I need a little time." He put his hand on Kent's shoulder. "Haven't I always had your back?"

"Yeah..."

"Then just give me some time to clean things up." Wade smiled. "Think of it as a paid vacation. You'll go up into the mountains, stay at a cabin for a while. I'll make sure you both have everything you want. Enjoy being out of the desert."

Kent nodded reluctantly. "All right. I can lay low for a month or two."

"Good man." Wade headed for the back entrance to the cells. "Follow me." He opened the door and the cool night air raced into the stuffy cells area.

There was a large, black SUV with tinted windows waiting outside. The rear door was open, and a mountain of a man stood beside it wearing a suit that was probably a size or two too small. Dwayne went straight into the vehicle and slid across the seat to the far side.

Kent paused, and looked back at the detective. "Don't leave me hanging out there. I'll be cool as long as I know what's going on."

Wade patted him on the arm. "You have my word that I'll keep you informed."

Kent jumped into the seat and the big man closed the door, then got up into the front.

The SUV pulled out of the station parking lot and its tail lights vanished into the night.

Wade turned to Spanky. "I wish I could kill that idiot myself."

"You just did." Spanky turned to head back inside. "It's my boys with their fingers on the knife-handle, that's all. Come on. We've got a call to make and the Mayor is waiting."

Rock pointed at the telephone receiver he was holding, and waved the two men in. Wade and Spanky obediently took their usual seats, and remained thankfully quiet.

"I understand you have to check on this," he said, "but the Blythe Bulletin isn't a real source of news. It's basically just one guy writing a blog. There's no way to verify any of the things he put in his story. For all we know, the woman in the mask beat up two random citizens and then staged the whole thing to make herself popular. She may even be working with the blogger to make it happen."

The voice on the phone made a horrifying suggestion.

He winced. "No, I'm definitely not saying that's what happened, and you can't quote that as my official version of events. I'm saying we have no way of knowing who's telling the truth at this time, and I was illustrating that *fact* with another, more plausible scenario that fits the circumstances as we know them. Our best investigators are looking into events, and we're hoping to find the girl to ask her some questions."

The caller insinuated several disturbing ideas.

"No. I'm not going to call her that. I don't want to legitimize any fantasies that this girl seems to be under. She's neither a vigilante nor a superhero, but a young woman who—at best—is putting herself into very real danger, and at worst is harming innocent people out of a pathological need for attention. I'm confident that the people of this city will call the police immediately if they happen to see her, and keep their distance. She needs to be helped before anyone else gets hurt."

Apparently, that was all the caller needed.

"All right, thank you for calling." Rock put the phone back on the cradle, then flicked the ringer to silent and rubbed the bridge of his nose. It was almost midnight and the phone hadn't stopped ringing in hours. He turned to his visitors. "What the *fuck* happened, Wade? I told you to stand down. All you had to do was lay low and let the local circus forget about a dumb girl in a makeshift Halloween costume. Instead she's suddenly dressed in high tech tactical gear and outing your officers on national news. You do understand that this is a monumental fuck-up, right?"

The detective squirmed in his seat. "It was Palmer. He didn't like being disrespected. He took it on himself to send the park a message."

"*Palmer* did this on his own?" Rock looked from Wade over to the other man.

Spanky gave a slight shrug, and rolled the toothpick from one side of his mouth to the other and then back.

The mayor shook his head and let out a long sigh. "I count on you to keep your... men in check, Wade." He glared at the detective. "This is a mess that is going to take a lot of work to clean up. But before we even try, can you promise me that nothing like this is going to happen again? You won't let anyone do anything without running it by me first?"

"Well, I didn't let him do it," Wade insisted. "But yeah, I can keep a tighter lid on things." He paused, his face suddenly vicious. "As long as that bitch gets taken care of."

Rock turned to Spanky. "You said earlier you've got an idea for that?"

"Yeah. I know a guy. About as dependable as you can get. But he ain't cheap."

"I don't think we have a choice." Rock stood up. "You need to use my computer to reach him, right?"

Spanky got up, and switched seats with him. Once the mobster was settled behind the keyboard, he opened a browser and typed in an I.P. address. "Your PC is completely secure, the most bulletproof in town. I had a guy make sure of that a while back. To reach this guy I have to go through a cloaking site from a secure machine, then log onto his page with a password that changes every thirty minutes."

Wade leant forward to try to see the screen. "If it changes so often, how do you know what it is?"

"Mathematical equation based on six different variables, including the time of day." Spanky was typing numbers furiously into his phone. "This guy is kind of a genius. Adapts his approach specifically to the problem, never using the same solution twice. Ah, here we go." He turned to the keyboard.

Rock glanced over and saw a symbol pop up on the computer screen—a red circle with eight red arrows stretching out from the circle, equally spaced around it. All of the arrows were an equal distance from the circle except the ones at 3 o'clock and 6 o'clock, which were much longer—a variation of the chaos symbol.

A second after the symbol appeared, a deep, raspy voice sounded from the speakers. "Good Evening, Mr. Spinello. I had a feeling you'd be reaching out."

Spanky pointed at the red 'active' light on the webcam. "Things have gotten interesting out here. Could use some help quieting it down again."

"I'm aware of the situation. Mr. Carrington is doing an admirable job trying to put the fire out."

Rock fought down a sudden wave of uncertainty. "Thank you."

Spanky grimaced impatiently. "Our concern is to prevent another sighting of the subject. She's gaining a bit of a following here, and that's going to cause some issues for our long-term plans."

"I've already been giving it some thought. What you need is a super villain."

Rock's eyes went wide. "I'm sorry, what?"

"The people of your city are looking at her as a hero," the voice declared. "They see her as a symbol of hope. But if her presence there brings in someone far worse—someone who causes a lot of damage and perhaps a certain amount of loss of life—then the city will turn on her. Then when she's finished and you apparently drive me off, *you* will be the hero."

Wade's head spun. "Wouldn't making her disappear work just as well? If she wasn't around anymore, people would forget about her."

"It's past that point," the speakers growled. "You'd make her a martyr. You can't just cut off the flower. You have to dig down into the dirt and pull it up by the roots. That is the way I solve problems."

Spanky nodded at the camera. "And we appreciate that. How soon can you take care of this?"

"I need to have an appropriate costume made. Three days, at the most. You won't hear from me again until it's done. I'll come to your city and engage with The Sting. Keep your officers and men away, so that I do not have to kill them to maintain appearances, understood?"

"Of course. How much ..." The computer screen went blank before Spanky could finish his question.

Rock stared at the computer. "That guy is bat-shit crazy."

"But he gets the job done." Spanky got to his feet and moved out from behind the desk.

"At what cost?" Rock slowly made his way back to his seat. "Is he going to come barreling in here with a tank, blowing everything to hell until she shows up? What have we unleashed?"

Spanky popped a fresh toothpick into his mouth. "The solution to our problem. Sure, he's unique, but he always gets the job done. Don't stress it, man. He's a professional."

Professional what? "Okay. Look, both of you, go home, get some sleep." Rock gestured at the door. "It'll probably be fine. I mean, it can't be much worse than what we're dealing with now, right?"

Wade and Spanky left, and once the door was closed, Rock pulled open the bottom drawer of his desk to reveal a bottle of Jack Daniels and a rocks glass. He poured himself a double, stared at it for a second, then filled the glass to the brim. He took a swig, grimacing at the burning sensation in the back of his throat, then tossed back the rest of it. Putting the glass down, he shut off his computer.

"It used to be so easy to run this city." A cold little voice in the back of his head whispered that it was going to get a lot harder real soon.

CHAPTER TEN

For several hours, Erin just sat at the truck stop Robert had left her at. The last few weeks, she'd just been winging it, one moment at a time. After dropping the shooters off with Bernie though, she'd felt really good—she had a job and a purpose, and it seemed like things might finally turn around. She'd had hope, for the first time since she'd come home from the Middle East. That hope had evaporated in Robert's truck. Now she was slumped in a cramped booth, eating chicken strips and feeling completely lost. Again.

Moving out to Indio had occurred to her a few times since her return. It was bigger than Blythe—almost four times the population—and it had casinos, golf courses, and other places people liked to spend money. Plus it was next to Coachella, which brought all the hottest music groups to the area. It wasn't Los Angeles or San Francisco, but for the middle of the desert, Indio wasn't too bad.

She wasn't sure why she'd never made the move. But even though things had felt hopeless in Blythe, she hadn't felt alone. She felt very alone now. But that was for later. Her immediate needs were a place to stay, a job, and somewhere safe to hide the suit. The suit. She tried not to groan. *Should it go back to Mr. Johnson?* It was custom made to fit her, and unless there was another female ex-soldier with serious anger issues in town, there wasn't much he could do with it. That was a good excuse to keep it, at least.

The truck stop employees weren't specially encouraging about a cheap room or places to apply for work. The tourist season had a few more months left, so rooms would still be sparse, but the work would be drying up for the same reason. While there was some year-round agriculture, the temperatures got over a hundred degrees on average from June to September, driving the tourists away.

Her best lead seemed to be the resort, which apparently had a lot of staff turn-over. Working at the casino appealed to her— her military background might help her catch on as security. Hell, she could even see herself as a dealer. She hoped it wouldn't come to working as a waitress or bell-hop, though. Not that those jobs were beneath her. Quite the contrary. *She* wasn't up to *their* standards. It was all too likely that she'd lose her cool and get fired. *You've got to know your limitations.*

She would have headed over there immediately, except it was well after midnight, and H.R. departments tended not to work graveyard shifts. That meant cooling her heels. The girl at the cash register offered to drop her off at the resort when she got off work at seven a.m. Everyone there was being very nice to her in fact, letting her just hang out even though she didn't have a vehicle. It helped that she'd lied a little and told the cashier that her boyfriend had dumped her there with almost no money and no-one to call for help. That had won her a lot of sympathy, especially as the story filtered through to the other employees. The chicken strips had been a gift, a wrong order by a drive-thru customer according to the cook. But, in fairness, Robert was a boy, and her friend, and he had dumped her there with no-one to call.

She leaned back in the booth and closed her eyes. With a few hours to kill, sleep was probably a good idea. Army life had taught her to sleep just about anywhere in any noise, including the inside of a helicopter. The swirling blades of a Huey were far louder than any mostly-empty truck stop. Blocking out instrumental versions of Imagine Dragons songs did take a lot more work than she'd expected though. She put her legs up on the opposite seat, against her duffle bag, so she'd feel it if anyone tried to take it. Then she folded her hands on her chest and took a long, deep breath. Two minutes later she was asleep.

Erin was jarred awake by a loud, screeching sound followed by a thunderous boom. She was on her feet and heading towards the door before the handful of people in the truck stop had started to react. The freeway was two hundred yards to the south, but even at that distance, the light of the full moon showed her that something bad had happened.

"Call 911!" she yelled back to the cashier, before pushing through the front doors.

As she ran past the gas pumps and towards the freeway, she could make out the silhouette of an overturned tanker truck. But it wasn't flat on the ground. The angle it sat at told her that it was on something. Then she saw a new light source flicker to life, and forced herself to run faster. She crossed the on-ramp and dashed up the embankment to the westbound side of interstate 10, and discovered that her worst fears had been realized.

A full-sized diesel with a tanker trailer full of gas had flipped over onto a mini-van. The diesel cab was on fire, tilted sideways. The passenger door was jammed shut, and the driver's door was pointed up at almost a seventy-five-degree angle.

She could see the truck driver struggling to get free of his seat belt. He was a good-sized man, and his weight was pinning him against the release. The mini-van was in horrible shape. The front had been flattened, the driver's space almost level with the crumpled hood.

The truck driver was the better bet.

She ran over and jumped onto the roof of the truck, then pulled herself up until she was perched on the driver's side of the cab. She pulled open the door. The man was still struggling.

He looked up at her with mixed hope and terror. "I can't get it loose!"

She fished through her pockets until she found the knife that her dad had always carried. "I want you to twist towards me as best you can, and grab the edge of the door jamb. I'm going to cut the belt loose, and we'll pull you out."

The man turned as instructed, one hand grabbing the door jamb, the other holding on to the steering wheel. He put his right foot against the open glove compartment, and nodded. Cutting through the belt took a few tries, like sawing through a tree branch, but when it finally tore through, the belt sprung down. The driver almost dropped to the other side of the cab. Erin managed to grab his arm and kept him from losing his grip on the door jamb. She heaved as he found foot-holds to lever himself up through the door.

She helped him slide down the roof to the ground, then followed. Checking him over, she found that his head was bleeding from where he'd hit the side window, and his left leg looked broken. A few cracked ribs would likely be found later, from the seat belt. She helped him hobble towards the shoulder, and saw the cook from the truck stop coming over to help.

"Get him down the embankment," she told him. "This whole thing is going to blow."

The guy took the driver's weight off Erin's shoulder. "What are you going to do?"

"I need to check the mini-van."

She was running back to the accident site when heard sirens fast approaching. A California Highway Patrol car screeched to a halt, and a tall, blond man leapt out carrying a fire extinguisher.

"The driver is out of the truck," Erin yelled to the officer. "I'm going to check on the van."

"I'll work on the fire, buy you some time!" he yelled back, already running. "More help is on the way!"

She stopped by the van for long enough to assess what was in front of her. The tanker was resting on the front driver's side. Smoke was now billowing across the scene, making it almost impossible to see inside. The rear passenger-side door was the only one that looked like it might come open, but even it was bowed out at the top, where the roof had been bent by the weight of the tanker.

She tried the handle. Thankfully, it was unlocked, but the door only moved half an inch. The frame was warped. She peered inside the window again, and couldn't make anything out for sure... but she thought she saw something move.

Bracing her foot up against the back tire for leverage, she pulled on the door with every ounce of strength she had. Nothing happened. She kept pulling, readjusting her grip, and then pulling more. Her muscles were starting to burn, but she kept pulling. The door shifted a little, maybe an inch. Progress. Ignoring the pain, she adjusted her stance again, took a deep breath and yanked as hard as she could... and the door swung open.

A small black and brown chihuahua leapt out of the mini-van and started barking at her.

She was about to say a few choice words about risking explosive death to save a dog when she heard a muffled cry from inside. Buckled onto the back seat, just inches below the crushed roof, was a baby's car seat. She quickly cut it free and pulled it out of the car. An unconscious toddler was bundled up inside. The crying came again, so she looked back inside and found a little girl tucked down on the floor of the car, behind the driver's seat. She was wedged in as tight as could be, with a jacket over her mouth to try and keep the smoke out.

Erin reached her hand in. "Come on, sweetie. Time to go."

The little girl hesitated. Her tear-stained eyes looked up at the front of the mini-van. The passenger seat was reclined.

Erin stretched further in, until she could almost touch the little girl. "Please, sweetie. It's not safe here. Let me help you."

The little girl finally reached out, and Erin gently but quickly pulled her out of the vehicle. She scooped the girl up in her right arm, picked up the baby seat in her left hand, and sprinted back towards the embankment. The barking dog followed. By the time she got there, the cook was running back up again. No words were needed this time. She passed him the children and immediately turned to run back to the accident.

About halfway there, the officer intercepted her. "The fire is spreading too fast. This whole thing is going to blow any second."

"The passenger had the seat reclined." She pulled away from him. "They might still be alive."

Erin raced back to the mini-van. The officer paused for a brief second, then ran after her. They found a woman wedged in between the seat and the crushed roof. There wasn't enough room to move her.

The officer checked for a pulse. "She's alive, somehow. I'm going to make some room. Try to pull her out." He lay flat on the ground, reached into the vehicle and grabbed the back of the seat.

He pulled the seat down, and just a little more room opened up. Erin slid her hands under the unconscious woman's arms, and pulled. As she did, she used her elbow to push down on the seat as well, to force it down a little more. It was a painstakingly long process, but once the woman's hips were clear, the officer sprung to his feet, and together they pulled the woman into his arms. Then they turned and sprinted for the embankment.

Scared they'd waited too long, Erin and the officer slid down the embankment, keeping the woman as safe as possible. Erin fully expected to hear the truck blow as they descended. It didn't. When they got to the bottom, the cook and a few others from the truck stop were there to help them carry the survivor to the other side of the onramp. More sirens wailed in the distance.

The officer turned to Erin and smiled. "Seems we had a bit more..."

The truck exploded with an Earth-shattering kaboom.

Erin's ears were still ringing when the paramedics and ambulances showed up. She watched firemen put out the tanker truck, feeling horrible that she hadn't been able to save the driver of the mini-van. Both children seemed to be okay once they got some oxygen to clear out the smoke. The woman, their mom, regained consciousness, but she'd suffered some severe breaks to her legs. The paramedics said that it would take her a long time to fully recover. The little dog never stopped barking, still audible even as all of them were in an ambulance and being driven off towards a local hospital. The truck driver had a concussion, a broken leg, and three cracked ribs. The officer tried to find out from him how the accident had happened, but Erin didn't really care.

The sun was just peeking over the horizon when the tanker truck was finally towed away, and the freeway reopened for business. The blond officer was the last one on the scene, and came over to Erin once everything had been taken care of.

"I know that look." He stood next to her, and together they stared at the early morning traffic. "You saved four people, and all you can think about is the fifth."

"That obvious, huh?"

He smiled. "To a trained professional, yes. We both saw how badly that van was crushed. The driver was gone before you reached the freeway. Don't beat yourself up over it. In everyone else's book, you're a hero."

"I'm nobody's hero." She turned to head back to the truck stop.

"There are four people at the hospital right now that would say otherwise." He paused. "And a dog."

Erin smiled. "Saving that dog is the part I feel the guiltiest about." She waved goodbye, and headed off.

When she got back to the truck stop, she found that the cashier had pulled her duffle bag behind the counter. "I didn't want anyone to mess with it. Troy told me everything you did. You're amazing."

She looked over and saw that the cook was back in his kitchen area. "Troy helped a lot. He's a good man."

The cashier smiled at that. "He'll make you some breakfast, and then I can drive you over to the casino."

Erin put a bottle of water and an energy bar on the counter. "I appreciate that a lot, but... I think I'm going to go a different direction."

The cashier grabbed a second bottle of water and two more energy bars, put them in a bag, and handed them to Erin. "On the house."

"Thanks." She smiled and took the bag, then threw her duffle over her shoulder and left the truck stop.

As she walked towards the highway ramp, she thought about the whole hero thing. *Was* she a hero? On multiple occasions, she'd risked her life to help others. But wasn't that just being a good person? Surely it should be just being a good person. She didn't feel like a hero, just someone who wanted to do the right thing.

Besides, heroes always rode off into the sunset. She was about to try to hitchhike her way towards the dawn, and that was completely different.

CHAPTER ELEVEN

Bernie sat at his desk, scanning the web for information about body armor. The design of the Sting's new suit was fascinating, but surely having it so skin-tight would sacrifice protection for looks? But why use a full-face mask if looks were a concern? Contradictions like that made his teeth itch. They were one of his pet journalistic peeves, and he knew he'd be worrying away at it until he had an answer. Along with the horde of other questions he'd been wrestling with since their meeting the night before. Like how could she afford a suit like that if she was based in Blythe, and why she'd come to him with the gunmen, and whether she'd chosen her name because of the British singer or the Paul Newman movie. The truth was, he could probably ask her a hundred questions and only make a small dent in the list of things he wanted to know.

This was someone who had decided to risk her life to help other people. What was in it for her? It wasn't fame or fortune, not when she was keeping her identity hidden. So did she have family or friends she was trying to protect? Was she getting revenge for something? Or was she just crazy? Okay, she probably *was* crazy, but surely that wasn't all there was to it. And above all, why Blythe? That was probably the question he came back to the most. Why was she standing up for a small town that everyone else seemed to have forgotten?

A knock at the door interrupted his musings. "Come in!" he called

The door opened to admit George, the mail guy. He popped in every day, a little after noon, with a big smile and a handful of flyers and ads. Sometimes, he actually had a bill in an honest-to-god addressed and stamped envelope. That was all the mail really was anymore. No one sent letters. It was all people wanting money, one way or another. When had Bernie received something in the mail he'd actually been happy to get? He couldn't even remember.

"You getting a new employee?" George asked.

The box holding the new flat-pack desk leaned against the far wall, where Bernie had dumped it earlier. It was a match to his own. If they went back to back, there ought to still be room for the two guest chairs at the end. It would make his office seem smaller, but it would be nice to have someone other than a loquacious mailman to talk to during the day.

"I think so." He leaned back in his chair, ready for their daily chat. "I made an offer. We'll see if they show up."

"Is this because of that vigilante chick?" The mailman examined the boxed desk. "I read your column this morning about her coming here. You think things are going to get busier now?"

Bernie nodded. "I hope so."

George turned back with a serious look on his face. "You sure getting involved with her is a good idea? Seems like the type of thing that invites trouble."

That gave him a moment's pause. "I'm here to report the news," he said finally. "Blythe deserves that, and the Sting is news. I'd be covering her whether she brought me trouble or not."

"I don't know... Vigilantes calling at your doorstep, now envelopes with no return addresses." He placed the mail on the desk. "That sort of thing can start to snowball."

The legal-sized envelope bore Bernie's name and address, handwritten in thick black ink. He picked it up and examined it. Other than the postage, there was nothing else on it. He started to open it.

"Wait." George took a few hasty backward steps towards the door. "Nothing personal, but, well, you're starting to mess with things that might not be healthy. I'd prefer to not be in the building when you open that package."

'It's an envelope, not a package."

"You've never heard of anthrax? Good luck, man." George dashed out the door, pulling it shut behind him.

Bernie shook his head and smiled. At least George's visit had been short for a change. He pulled at the corner of the envelope, then stopped and shook it self-consciously, listening for any loose powder. Nothing. He tore the end open. Inside was a single sheet of paper that looked like something out of the *X-Files*. It was a copy of a letter to the governor of California, and referenced something called Project: Camelot. The letter mentioned Blythe, and there were a few other words visible, but the majority of the text was blacked out like a top-secret document. He turned the page over, hoping for more, but it was blank. If someone was trying to give him a clue, it was about as vague as you could make it. There wasn't even a hint regarding what it pertained to.

He turned to his computer and pulled up new tab. He'd started typing in 'Project Camelot' when he was interrupted by his phone ringing.

"Blythe Bulletin."

A raspy, muffled voice replied, "You'll want to send someone to the bank right away."

He blinked. "Which bank?"

There was a pause, and a nasty crackle. "This pissant town has more than one bank?"

"We have four. There's Bank of—"

The caller interrupted. "The one where the Sting stopped the robbery."

"What does this have to do with her?"

There was a nasty laugh. "I'm calling out your local vigilante..." The line popped, and went dead.

Bernie stared at his phone for a long minute, unsure if he should take the caller seriously. He was still staring, lost in thought, when it rang again.

"Blythe—"

"God damn it." The raspy voice was back. "You have *really* shitty cell coverage here. I'm calling out your vigilante. If she doesn't meet me there in the next hour, I'm going to start killing people."

The phone clicked and the line dropped again.

Bernie dithered. They really *did* have horrible cell service, so he wasn't sure if the call was over or not. After two full minutes had passed, he figured it was probably safe to assume it was over. He locked the door to the office and headed out to his car. He was behind the wheel and about to turn the key when he realized he should probably call the cops.

There was a small crowd gathering in the parking lot adjacent to the bank. Bernie pulled up across the street, away from the fuss. There were about two-dozen people in semicircle over by the entrance, and a few more were headed that way. He hopped out of the car and dug out his cell-phone. He needed to film the whole thing, from first arrival through to whatever the caller had in mind. He started shooting and then crossed the street to merge with the people, pushing his way through until he could see what was going on.

Four people were kneeling on the ground with their hands behind their heads, two men and two women. He recognized them—the bank's employees. He'd spoken to them the day after the robbery. They were all understandably looking scared. The figure standing behind them was straight out of a comic book, a man dressed in black: jeans, boots, armored chest piece, full-face mask, and a long leather duster. The outfit was accented in red—a belt and holster, knee pads, forearm bracers, and a circle around his right eye with arrows of various length going in every possible direction. The symbol looked familiar, but he couldn't quite place it.

The guy was pacing back and forth, carrying a scary-looking gun. Bernie knew nothing about guns, but this one had a long magazine that curled like a banana, and a short stock. It was being wielded and he held it like a pistol, even though it looked more like a machine gun. He figured he could ask Erin later, if she took the job.

The man leaned down over one of the hostages. "Where the hell is she? I thought heroes were supposed to be punctual."

The hostage at the far left, the bank manager—Wilkes—spoke up nervously. "Maybe she hasn't heard that you're looking for her?"

The gunman moved to the end. "Well, how did you guys let her know you needed her before?"

"We didn't. She just showed up."

The masked man shook his head. "That doesn't make any sense. No one just *happens* upon a bank robbery. She had her costume on. She had to know somehow." He resumed his pacing.

That was when Bernie noticed a single police officer sneaking up from the back of the parking lot. He was making his way along the front of the cars on the left-hand side, using them to hide his movements, advancing one car each time the gunman paced away from him. It was painstakingly slow but effective. Eventually, the cop got directly in line with the gunman and crouched down, leaning his arms on the hood of a Toyota pick-up.

"Freeze, poli—"

The gunman whipped round and fired three shots in the blink of an eye. The bullets ripped into the officer, tearing into his chest, then his chin, and finally his forehead.. His body crumpled to the ground, leaving a bloody smear.

A low moan went through the crowd, and there were a few muffled screams. The hostages paled even further. Bernie swallowed, concentrating on not throwing up.

Spinning back round again on his heel, the killer snapped his fingers. "That's it! One of you two must be the Sting!"

He moved to crouch down between the two female hostages, looking at them intently. The one on his left, a young Asian woman, refused meet his gaze.

The one on his right, an older African-American woman, looked him straight in the symbol. "If you think I could get my ass in that costume I saw in the newspaper, you're even crazier than you look. And that's saying something."

The man shrugged, then turned to the Asian woman. "If it's you, then you might as well tell me now. Cause if the Sting isn't here in another ten minutes, I'm going to shoot one of you. And another one every ten minutes after that until she shows up. If that's you and you don't fess up, then I'm going to be killing a whole lot of people."

"You only have four hostages!" shouted a voice from the crowd.

The gunman stood and pointed his gun in that direction. "Oh, really? I see another couple of dozen just standing right in front of me. Which reminds me. If anyone tries to leave, I'm opening fire on all of you."

"I'm not her," the Asian woman finally said. "She saved me from the bank robbers."

"You've been a hostage twice now?" The gunman laughed. "You've got some rotten luck, lady."

There was no way of knowing what would happen if the Sting did—or didn't—show up. But the man in black and red had already killed one person as if swatting a fly. The threat had to be taken seriously.

Bernie switched his phone to live-stream, and then stepped forward out of the crowd, head spinning. "Bernie Green, Blythe Bulletin." *What the hell am I doing?*

"Oh, hey Bernie. Thanks for coming." The masked man gestured around himself. "What do you think of all this?"

"I think you're threatening to murder a lot of people, and you've already executed one cop. But you really haven't said *why*." He held up his camera, trying with all his might to keep his voice even. "I'm live-streaming this to my audience. Maybe you'd like to take this opportunity to tell everyone what brought you to this point?"

"Really?" The gunman took a couple steps forward, moving out past the hostages. "You think people will care? I mean, sure, the people here do because I'm threatening to kill them. But you think the people at home want to hear it?"

"Are you kidding? That is the most important part." Bernie made himself move in a step. "You don't want people to think you're just off your meds or something, right? I mean, you seem to have a strong desire to confront the Sting. Tell us where that comes from."

"Yeah, that would be great." He moved even closer to the camera, but kept his gun pointed at the crowd. "I grew up reading comic books. I loved them, but not because of the heroes. The whole idea of doing things because of responsibility, or for truth and justice, that seemed like a load of crap. But doing things to get rich, gain power, rule a country, get the girl, those were all reasons I could relate to. Reasons to put on a costume and become a villain. Now, I've done a lot of villainous things in my life. You can't imagine the number of bodies in shallow graves I've left scattered about this country. And while it was good, and I enjoyed the killing, the torturing, and all the money I got for doing it, none of it really felt like something a true supervillain would do."

Despite the horror and the fear, Bernie forced himself to nod encouragingly.

"But then I hear about the Sting. An honest-to-God costumed vigilante stopping bank robberies and taking out meth labs. And it clicked. *That's* what I was missing. You can't be a supervillain unless you have a superhero to go up against. That's what I've been missing my whole life. An archenemy. I put together this costume, came up with a name, and then figured out where the hell Blythe even was. That was the hardest part, truly. So here I am, ready to make a name for myself."

He's completely insane, but while he's talking, he's distracted. "You said you had a name?"

"Oh, right." The maniac struck a pose with his gun up, glaring into the camera. "I am Mister Chaos."

"Of course!" Bernie found himself pointing at the red symbol on the mask, and tried not to cringe back. "The chaos symbol."

"Yeah." Chaos leaned forward so the camera could see it better. "I adjusted it a bit, lengthening a couple of the arrows to make it my own. Branding is so key to being successful in just about anything these days."

"I took a seminar about branding—" Bernie babbled.

"Hang on." Chaos put up his hand, turned, and shot the other male hostage, the one who wasn't Wilkes, through the temple. Blood spurted, and the corpse sagged forward. The crowd erupted in screams and panicked shouts of denial. Bernie turned and vomited onto the road, dimly aware that he was not the only one. Chaos turned back around, and waited politely for Bernie to wipe his mouth off. "Sorry about that. We hit ten minutes past the hour. You were talking about a branding seminar?"

CHAPTER TWELVE

The truck's brakes squealed, waking Erin up, and the big rig crunched to a stop at the bottom of the off-ramp for Blythe's first exit. The driver was hauling a trailer full of vegetables towards Phoenix, and had picked her up just outside of Desert Center. He'd seemed harmless enough, and she'd been so worn out that she'd nodded off in the passenger seat. Now she was back, and he'd been as good as his word. She smiled at him and she stepped down out of the cab, dragging her duffle bag behind her.

"Thanks for the ride!" She called up. He waved and put the big truck back into gear as she closed the door.

She stood on the corner as he pulled away, trying to figure out her next move. First, she needed to check in with Bernie to see if she still had a job to take up. She couldn't really tell him why she hadn't shown up on time without revealing that she was the Sting, and she wasn't ready for anyone to know that. Well, except Robert, who wasn't even talking to her anymore, and Mr. Johnson, who was, at the very minimum, conspiring with her. She figured she'd go by and see the old man later. After that, she could sleep in her storage unit for a night or two while she figured out a place to stay. It wasn't ideal, but it was a start.

Which brought her back to Robert. *Avoid him or confront him?* If he wanted her out of his trailer, that was his decision. But the bullshit of driving her to another city was too much. What she did with her life wasn't for him to decide. It wasn't his job to protect her. But as much as she wanted to tell him all that, she didn't see what good it would do. He was just as stubborn as she was, and he'd made his feelings crystal clear.

She walked into the shop of the ramp's gas station to grab a water before starting the trek to the Bulletin. When she stepped inside, she saw that the cashier and both customers were just staring at the television behind the counter. She left her bag by the door, headed to the back to get her water, then went to pay. After a few second of being ignored, she finally glanced at the television.

A freaky-looking guy in a black mask was on the screen. "What the hell?"

"Some psycho has taken a bunch of hostages over at the bank," one of the customers told her. "Same one that got robbed. He's already killed two people, including a cop."

"Where the hell are the rest of the police?"

The cashier snorted. "You're kidding, right? If there was one good cop in this city, he was the one that maniac already shot."

"This is insane." She slid around the side to get a better look. "The masked guy brought his own camera?"

"He calls himself Mister Chaos. Says he wants to fight the Sting. The feed is coming from our local paper guy, although I bet every station in California has helicopters on the way."

"Bernie?" Erin grabbed her bag. "I need to borrow your bathroom."

The cashier tossed her a key that was attached to big piece of wood that said 'Women'.

She caught it out of the air, headed around the back of the building, and let herself in. The bathroom was surprisingly clean, with a small end-table in the corner holding a potted plant. She moved the plant to the floor, put her duffle bag up on the table and started pulling out the pieces of her suit. It went on easier now that she knew how it worked. She put the sticks on her back, dropped Wishmaster into its holster, and clicked her mask into place.

She stepped outside and looked to see if anyone was around. It was clear, with no security cameras. A quick climb up the propane tank cage gave her access to the ledge, where she could pull herself up far enough to swing the bag up onto the roof, out of sight.

Dropping back down, she started to run up Lovekin Avenue, heading for Hobson Way. It was only three miles. No worries. She just hoped that Mister Chaos didn't kill anyone else before she could get there to stop him.

As she ran under the freeway overpass, a motorcycle pulled up next to her. The rider lifted his visor and yelled at her, "Get on!" He stopped the bike and gestured behind him with his thumb.

She hesitated for a second, before swinging her leg over the seat and wrapping her arms around his waist. The guy cranked the throttle and shot off, ignoring a red light to drift into the turn onto Hobson Way. They raced down the street, zipping through traffic, and took a surprise left on Broadway before coming to a stop about a block up. The perfect spot to approach from behind the lunatic.

She hopped off the bike and leaned in, so she could be heard over the engine. "Perfect. Thanks!"

The biker flashed her a thumbs up. "Go get him, Sting!"

Erin nodded, turned and jogged towards the back of the insurance company on the opposite side of the parking lot from the bank. She dashed along the back of the building, and peeked around the corner. The scene hadn't changed much from what she'd seen on the television. Chaos was talking to Bernie, who was as white as a sheet, but still standing there in front of a crowd of people, holding his phone. But why were there so many people just watching a maniac with a gun?

The dead cop had clearly tried to sneak up, and it hadn't worked. There was another corpse, at the end of a hostage line. Chaos' shoulders twitched, and she ducked back immediately, dropping out of view just as he turned back towards the bank employees.

"She's got one more minute before I shoot another one of you." The gunman's voice was disguised, oddly hoarsened. It faded a bit, and she figured he'd turned back away from her, towards the crowd. "Or maybe I shoot one of you this time. Change things up a bit. I don't want to seem predictable."

The parking lot was too wide for her to sneak up on the psycho. Even if she could, someone in the crowd would probably see her and give her away. She could just shoot him, but at that distance, if he moved she'd end up killing someone in the crowd. It was at that moment she remembered the words of her high school math teacher, *When you have no choice, it's easy to make up your mind.*

She stood tall, took a deep breath, and walked out into the parking lot with as much confidence as she could muster. "Sorry I'm late. I had a hard time hitching a ride by the state prison."

The crowd erupted as Chaos spun on his heels, raising his gun up to fire. "You have any idea how long you've kept me waiting? I should just shoot you and be done with it."

"What would that prove?" Bernie moved to masked man's side, his face urgent. "You came here to prove yourself against our superhero. No one will be impressed if you shoot her before she's even pulled her gun. What do you want the world to say about Mister Chaos? Do you want to be known as a bad-ass fighter or a bully?"

Chaos glanced at the reporter. "You're a crazy little shit, aren't you? All right. I'll give you a show." The man dropped his gun to his side and slid it into a holster at the small of his back. He walked past the hostages towards her.

Behind him, Bernie was filming with one hand while frantically waving for the crowd to run away with the other. They followed orders, and scattered. The hostages bee-lined for the bank doors as Bernie moved past them, continuing to film.

As he walked, Chaos reached into his duster and pulled out a metal bar about two feet long. He stopped and held it out horizontally in front of him, in a fist. There was a soft click, and the bar expanded out in both directions, telescoping twice to become a solid, six-foot long staff. He spun it around twice then swung it behind him, taking an opening Bōjutsu stance.

Erin pulled her escrima sticks and swept them up into the first position in the Kali Heaven Six, right-hand stick over her shoulder, the other under the same shoulder with her arm across her body.

They circled around each other, like two tigers ready to strike. "What are you waiting for?" she asked. "You wanted this fight."

"I know." Chaos looked around the parking lot. "I was just thinking how much better this would be if there was some music blaring. A techno-instrumental with a heavy bass beat, maybe."

"I'm surprised you didn't bring a boom-box. Figured you had this all planned."

He fumbled through his duster until he found his phone. "This is the best I can do." He backed off warily a step or two and thumbed his phone for a bit before tucking it into his belt. A 90's techno song from a popular video-game franchise began playing, as a deep voice chanted about testing your might, and ordered them to fight.

A second later, Chaos had the staff whipping around towards her head. She dropped to one knee. The staff swung over her. She brought her right stick up to block the inevitable follow-up kick. It deflected harmlessly. She smacked the inside of his thigh with her left stick. It wasn't a serious blow, but would show she wasn't going to be a push-over.

He staggered back two steps, then returned to his opening position. "That's what I'm talking about. A real, honest-to-god vigilante. Not just some whack-job in a suit."

"You mean like you?" Erin was back on her feet and ready.

This time he stepped forward. He thrust the end of the staff towards her midsection. She'd seen this move before too. Deflecting left with her right hand would let him swing the back half of the staff around savagely. Instead, she stepped left and blocked with her left hand. His momentum pushed back onto him. Then she stepped forward and smashed him across the chest with her right stick.

"You bitch."

He took a step back. She pressed the advantage. Her sticks smacked the knuckles on both of his hands. His fingers would go numb for a few minutes. It would make staff fighting a bit more difficult. To his credit, he didn't drop the weapons. He did two quick feints, one from each end.

The phone suddenly changed tunes to a group of guys calling out to a young man, and assuring him that he didn't need to be down.

Erin blinked at the sudden and drastic shift in music. She wasn't ready when Chaos literally threw his staff at her. She used both sticks to knock it down, and that left her defenseless. The masked man stepped in and punched her in the face. The world jerked about wildly. Chaos kicked out hard, driving his boot into her midsection. The suit took some of the impact, but the blow still knocked the wind out of her. She felt her sticks tumbling to the ground.

He stepped into his next move, driving his knee up into her groin. Pain lanced through her, and she doubled over. A brutal smash hammered down onto the back of her neck. Her legs gave way, dropping her to her knees. Chaos darted around to kick her in the side. Her ribs screamed, and she fell, desperately twisting to land on her back, gasping for air.

"Can I get a still shot?"

Chaos turned to face the voice. "What?"

Bernie stepped forward, holding his camera. "You've got her beat. I'd love to have you pose over the body. I could get a great shot for the paper. The proud moment when the villain defeats the hero."

"That's not a bad idea." He put his boot on her chest and flexed his muscles. "How's this?"

"Perfect," Erin said, as she grabbed one of the sticks she'd dropped.

She swung the stick up hard into the maniac's exposed groin.

He staggered back. She scrambled to her feet, bringing the stick up and smacking him ferociously under the chin. His head bobbed and he wavered blearily. She cracked him across the face again. He spun around in a circle and bounced off a parked car to wobble back towards her. She dropped the stick, and punched him in the face as he lurched towards her. The blow knocked him off his feet, and he landed hard on his back, out cold.

She stood over his body and shouted, "That's why villains always lose. Because they're stupid!"

No sooner had Mister Chaos dropped than the sound of sirens began in the distance. Bernie switched off his camera, and ran over to the Sting. "*Now* the cops are coming."

"I've got to get out of here." She snatched up her escrima sticks.

"My car is across the street. I can drop you somewhere if you want."

Running through the city back to the gas station with the cops everywhere was a really bad idea. "That would be great."

They ran over to his car. The very few spectators that remained were staring at the unconscious lunatic and the corpses. Bernie opened the back door, and she threw herself in and down behind the seats, so the cops wouldn't see her. He got the car started and took off. No sirens chased after them.

"Where to?" he asked, looking at her in the rearview mirror.

"Behind the gas station on Lovekin and Donlon."

"Thanks for coming. I honestly think he would've kept shooting people until you arrived." His voice cracked a little. "I really didn't want to die."

"Then why didn't you run off with everyone else when the fighting started?"

"I had to get the story." He puffed up his chest. "I'm a reporter."

She smiled under her mask. "Well, you bought me the moment I needed to recover, and most likely saved my life. Today, you're the hero."

They drove the rest of the way in silence. When Bernie was certain no-one was watching, she got out, and he drove off quickly. She pulled herself up onto the roof, took off her mask, and lay there for a moment, her whole body aching like hell. Three questions burned in her mind. Where had that guy come from? Why did he actually want so much to fight her? And why the hell did he have to hit so hard?

CHAPTER THIRTEEN

Sore and tired from the confrontation with Mister Chaos, Erin removed all the accessories from her gear and tucked them into her duffle bag. She left the form-fitting base suit on though, just pulling her jeans and plaid shirt on over it. After lacing up her sneakers, she was ready to go, until a cop car pulled into the parking lot. She waited on the roof, keeping as low as possible while the car stopped and the officer got out. Once he was safely inside the store, she dropped back down to the ledge and climbed down the propane tank cage, leaving her bag behind, and followed him in.

The same kid was behind the counter, but the officer was the only customer. He was pouring himself a cup of coffee. She made her way towards the back, still wanting that bottle of water she'd originally come in for.

The cashier was talking to the cop. "What finally happened at the bank? The live-stream cut out before the end."

"It was all over by the time we got there." He was emptying several sugar packets into his cup at once. "The psycho was lying on the ground. Furlong swooped in and picked him up. We chased off the gawkers and that was it."

"What happened to the Sting? Anyone see where she went?"

"No idea." He dumped several more sugars into the cup. "We were told someone else would deal with witness statements. We just had to clear the area and get back to our patrols."

She grabbed a water and a granola bar, headed back up to the front, and put the items on the counter.

The cashier punched in some numbers, but he was far more interested in talking to the cop. "I thought you guys would want to talk to her or something?"

Three more sugar packets went into the cup simultaneously. "Blythe Police Department doesn't acknowledge the existence of the Sting and doesn't condone vigilante activity, and any further inquiries should be taken up with the Mayor's office."

The kid laughed as he took Erin's money and the key to the women's room. "Sounds like you got that memorized."

The officer brought his coffee cup to the counter and stood next to her. "That lunatic asshole killed one of ours, as well as a hostage, and the Sting took him down before anyone else got hurt. That puts her on our side in my book. What the higher-ups think, that's on them." He reached in his pocket for his money.

The cashier waved him off. Giving officers free coffee meant they came by your store more often, and that kept the place just a little bit safer. It was the policy in a lot of places. The cop thanked the kid and headed out the door while Erin got her change. As she walked out the door, the cruiser was pulling out onto the street. She waited until he was out of sight, then retrieved her bag and started walking.

The exercise felt good. When she'd first set out, the places where Chaos had hit her had begun to tighten up and get sore. But the constant movement kept the blood flowing, and started the healing process. She would ache tomorrow, that was for damn sure, but she would still be able to move. When she got to the trailer park, she had to remind herself not to turn left and head for Robert's trailer. She didn't live there anymore, and she wasn't ready to deal with him.

She went up the center road instead, to Mr. Johnson's place. As she approached, she saw that he'd taken pieces of duct tape and covered the holes where the bullets had ripped through the steel sides of the trailer. She thought about it for a second and barked a short chuckle of disbelief at how much had happened in a day. The suit, the drive-by shooting, the gun men, Bernie, Robert banishing her to Indio, the truck accident, hitchhiking back, and then the confrontation with Mister Chaos to top it off. She suddenly felt very tired and desperately in need of a beer.

She knocked on the trailer door and heard movement inside. A second later the old man opened the door and burst into a big smile. "You've had a hell of a day. Want a drink?"

"Yes." She stepped in and closed the door behind her. "And you don't even know the half of it."

She took a seat at the table and leaned her head back against the wall behind her. Johnson busied himself around the kitchen for a minute before coming back to the table with a bottle, two glasses and a bowl of potato chips. The bottle was Artemis bourbon and had the silhouette of a woman pulling back a bow on it. He poured two healthy measures over ice and slid a glass over to her. She snatched it up, gestured with it towards him, and then drank half the glass in one shot. The alcohol burned over her tongue with a scent like Novocain, and then left a nice, warm sensation that ran down her throat and into her body.

"How did the suit work out?" He took a sip of his drink.

"It's incredible. I can move well in it, it definitely absorbs a chunk of the impact, and its light enough to wear under street clothes if I take off the extras. If I didn't know better, I'd start thinking this isn't your first vigilante outfit."

The old man laughed. "My first for an actual vigilante. What happened with the guy in the mask?"

"I got distracted and he took advantage." She chomped on a few chips. "I wasn't ready for just how crazy he was. I've dealt with soldiers and fanatics, but never that sort of lunatic."

"From what I could see on the TV, the guy was wearing some body armor himself. Mostly standard military grade, nothing on par with what you're wearing, but enough to deflect some of your attacks. I figured you're you'd be going up against street trash, not costumed villains. I'll have to do some upgrades. Maybe build a Taser into your sticks."

"Upgrades?" Erin shook her head. "I'm still getting used to what you gave me."

He topped off their glasses. "Can I see the mask?"

She pulled it out of the bag and handed it to him. He ran his fingers along the jaw line until he hit what looked to be a little notch that she hadn't noticed before. When he pressed it, a small piece of plastic extended out—an SD memory card that he removed.

"What is that?" she asked, genuinely surprised.

He pulled his laptop over from the side of the table and inserted the card. "When the mask is locked into place, it records your vital signs. It also monitors the rest of the suit for impact pressure, reduction rates, body temperature and about a dozen other stats."

"My dad was a decade younger than you and he couldn't even get his phone to link to his wireless router. How do you know all this stuff?"

"I've always liked playing with technology." A couple of charts popped up on his screen. "Your heart rate was remarkably steady through the whole fight. Even when he had you on the ground. That's amazing."

"Tell that to my ex-roommate who says I have anger issues." She took another gulp of the bourbon.

"Ex-roommate? You're not staying with Robert anymore?" He topped her glass off again.

"No. The asshole decided to banish me because of what I'm doing." She paused and took a deep breath. "He thinks that I'm putting myself and others in danger through my actions. That these things are happening because I went after the meth lab. And maybe he's right—but it feels like I'm starting to help some people. Bad things have been happening in this city for a while now, and it seems that all I'm doing is bringing it to the surface. Shining a light on it."

"This town has been beaten down by everything from technology to time." Johnson leaned back in his chair. "Blythe was going to be a big resort town in the early 1800s, but the main investor died before it got very far along. Then the city was built up in the early 1900s as part of the railways, but with planes and cars, no one cares much for trains anymore. Now we're the last city in California before going into Arizona. The place you drive through to get cheaper gas over the border. The people here struggle to get by, while anyone with any power just uses it to line their own wallets."

She looked him in the eye. "Why are you here?"

"I was born here. During World War II, my father spent part of his time stationed here, at the Air Force facility at the Gary Field. Working on some experimental equipment." He held up the mask. "I kind of followed in his footsteps."

He turned to work on his laptop for a minute, so she grabbed another handful of chips to munch on. There was a lot more to this old guy, and she was determined to find it all out. Only not just yet. She was too tired. She wanted to finish up here then go get some sleep. In the morning she would go check with Bernie and see if she still had a job. Everything else, she'd figure out later.

He pulled the memory card out of his computer and clicked it back into the mask, then handed the mask back to her. "It's ready to go. I can study the rest of the data later."

"Sounds good." She tucked it back into the bag and got to her feet. "I appreciate the drink."

"Where are you staying?"

She thought about lying, given how pitiful the truth sounded, but there was no point to it. "I've got a storage unit next to the trailer park. I'll stay there."

"You're kidding, right?" He got up and headed back into the kitchen, where he started rummaging through a small drawer.

"No, that's pretty much my plan," she admitted. "At least until I find out if I have a job or not."

Johnson returned and put a key down on the table. "Green and white trailer, one street over. Third from the end."

"What about it?"

"Its yours now." His tone was matter of fact.

She stared at him. "Wait, what? You can't just give me a trailer."

"Sure I can." He sat back down. "It used to belong to Wanda Avery, a lovely woman in her sixties who passed away at the Sizzler while enjoying their all-you-can eat salad bar. Her only living relative was a cousin named Walter, who flew out to box up her things and clean out the trailer. He tried to sell it, but he couldn't find any buyers, and he didn't see a reason to keep paying space rental on it, so he gave it to me."

"Why would he do that? Were you friends with Avery?"

"Enough to, say, wave hello in passing, that's about it." He used his hand to make a circle over his head. "I own all of this."

"The trailer? So?"

"No." He smiled. "The park. And the storage facility next door. My father invested in the area when he was out here. I inherited it, along with a few other pieces of land. Walter gave me the trailer to cover some back rental that Wanda owed. I had no intention of charging him for it, but he wanted to be square."

"And you're letting me stay in it? That's—"

"Nah." He pushed the key towards her. "You can have it. Easier for me to help you with the suit if you're close by. Don't get too excited though. It's an old unit and it needs work, but it's better than sleeping in storage."

She picked up the key, and gave him a genuine smile. "It really is. Thank you."

The green and white trailer was fifty feet long. It had the kitchen at one end, with a small table, and then a living room area. That led to a hallway with a small bedroom that Wanda had turned into an office / storage area, then a bathroom, and finally the master bedroom. All of Wanda's personal items had been removed, but there was furniture inside that looked serviceable. Hell, it would be great to have an actual bed to sleep on after months of being on a couch.

Erin felt utterly exhausted, and would have instantly fallen asleep if she'd laid down, but she didn't want to. Instead, she took her bag to the back bedroom, and started doing something she hadn't done in a very long time—unpack.

The pieces of the suit went into the middle room, in one of the built-in cabinets. Her jeans and shirts went onto some of the two-dozen plastic hangers that had been left in the main bedroom closet. She didn't have enough clothes to use them all, but there were a few shirts that escaped her bag for the first time in half a year. Socks and underwear went in a drawer. Her extra pair of shoes got tucked under the bed.

It didn't take her long. She placed the picture of her father on top of the dresser, making a mental note to go by the Dollar store and buy a frame for it. There was a clock radio by the bed, and a few turns of the dial tuned into a classic rock station. Her hips swung side to side a bit as she moved through the trailer.

Over the next couple of days, she could go to the storage unit and get some more things out. She'd also go by the grocery store and pick up some food, since she actually had a working refrigerator suddenly. How much food she *did* buy would depend on her visit to the Blythe Bulletin in the morning, but she'd be able to get up and shower before heading over there. Which was way better than if she had slept in the storage unit like she'd planned.

She was on her fifth or sixth trip through the living room when it suddenly hit her. She stopped and looked around where she was standing. In a very short amount of time, she had made a decision to try and help someone. While it hadn't gone as planned, and it had led to a whole heap of insanity in a very short amount of time, it had also brought her to a new place in her life. She was thinking of tomorrow. Making *plans*. She had a future, and it didn't feel like the world was beating her down. So much had changed, so quickly.

For the first time since leaving the service, she had a reason to get up in the morning and a place to call home.

CHAPTER FOURTEEN

Rock stormed through the police station, rage burning white-hot inside him. How had things gotten so far out of control? Just two weeks ago, the town had been running like clockwork. Everything had been lined up perfectly. Another six months, and he could have gone anywhere in the world. A cabin in Aspen. A beach in Barbados. A five-star hotel in Paris. Then some moron decided to become a vigilante. He could've dealt with a one-time anomaly, if Furlong had only been able to keep himself in check. Then that lunatic Spanky'd called in had blown everything to hell. *Maybe I should just pack my stuff and leave town. Walk away before it got any worse.* He couldn't do it though. Not with that much money on the table, not if there was even a slim a chance he could still get things back under control. The first urgent task was to take care of Mister Chaos.

A young officer walked past.

"Where's Detective Furlong?" he barked at her.

She flinched, then quickly turned and pointed at one of two gray doors along the back wall of the main office.

The mayor bulled straight for the door. He didn't bother to knock, he just smashed down the handle, and strode into the observation area for the interrogation set up that the department had put in a year back. The room was barely bigger than a broom closet. In fact, it *had been* a broom closet before they put in the two-way mirror, and offices supplies were still stacked on the opposite wall from the glass. Furlong was leaning against the window's ledge and staring through into the other room, where Mister Chaos sat quietly at a table, drinking a can of orange soda.

Rock forced his anger down a notch, shut the door, and took a place next to the detective. "What's he said so far?"

"Just that he'd only talk once you got here." Furlong kept staring. "He's on his third orange soda."

"What, you run out of coke?"

81

"Nope. He specifically wants orange." Furlong shook his head. "How fucked are we?"

"If your wife, girlfriend and mistress all showed up at your surprise birthday party, it would still be less fucked than this." The mayor opened the door into the interrogation room. "But like that scenario, if we play our cards right we can get everything we want. Let's see if we can fix this."

The two men moved into the second room and closed the door behind them. Chaos nodded to them as they walked in. He still wore his mask, but he'd pulled it up over his mouth and nose so that he could drink the soda. The guy looked Caucasian, with the beginnings of a dark five-o'clock shadow. The only distinguishing mark was that one of his central incisors—top right—was chipped at a thirty-degree angle. It wouldn't have been obvious, except that the guy's mouth was all Rock could see.

Chaos drained the last of his soda and put the can on the table. He crushed it with an elbow strike so fast and brutal that it made Rock jump back. The killer smiled. "Could I get another?"

Furlong turned and looked for approval. Rock nodded, and the detective left the room. The mayor sat down in one of the open chairs across from the masked man and tried to regain his composure.

The man on the other side of the table was insane. No matter how good his reputation was, the guy put on a costume and killed a cop while a reporter live-streamed the whole thing. He was so into his role that he hadn't taken his mask or even his gloves off after getting arrested. It was like the stories you heard about actors getting so into character that they slept in a barn next to their horse, or took up drugs just to live the part the whole time. The guy was absolutely crazy... Unless—he wasn't.

The possibilities hit the mayor like a ton of bricks.

Furlong returned with the new orange soda and placed it on the table. "That's the last one."

"Send one of the deputies to get more." Rock gestured to the mirror behind him. "Then wait in the observation room and make sure no one is watching us. Tap twice on the window when it's secure."

"And can you get me some Nutter Butters?" Chaos smiled, and popped open the can of soda. "The full cookies, not the little bites they put out now."

Furlong looked confused, but Rock just nodded at him again, so he shrugged and went to do as he was told.

Chaos waved at his soda can. "Want a sip?"

"I'm good, thanks," Rock said.

The other man nodded pleasantly, and took a deep drink. Silence descended, and Rock studied his fingernails impatiently until there was a double rap on the glass behind him.

The mayor gathered his thoughts. "Is this going as you planned?"

Chaos pulled his mask off. He was a ruggedly handsome man, probably in his early thirties. His black hair was trimmed close to the sides and back of his head, while the top was longer and stylishly messy. He had a square jaw, strong cheek bones, and a perfectly straight nose that looked like an after-shot in a rhinoplasty ad. His looks were offset by an inch-long scar that cut vertically down over his left eye, slashing through the brow and eyelid beneath. The pupil was milky white. He'd have stuck in the memory even without the left eye issues, but as it was, he was totally unforgettable.

"Almost." The man rolled his head and popping sounds came from his neck. "I'd planned to beat the snot out of her and leave her for the police. But she was better trained than I expected. I won't make that mistake again."

"Again?" Rock looked around them. "You're in jail. How do you expect to fight her again?"

"I'm going to break out tonight and do something crazy to get her attention. She'll come find me immediately." He leaned back in his chair. "That's the thing about heroes—they're ridiculously predictable."

"You say that like we're in some sort of comic book with caped crusaders in every city. To the best of my knowledge, the Sting is the first person to actually imitate those freaks, and you've been hired to make her the last."

Chaos shook his head. "This isn't about the Sting, but the situation that created her. She is an extreme response to the socioeconomic inequality that permeates the country. Blythe happens to be a perfect microcosm of government corruption escalating to an untenable point."

"You're saying she's a direct response to what we're doing?" Rock took a few seconds to think that over carefully. "I don't see it. Everything we've done has been gradual. She came out of nowhere and became a huge pain in my ass almost overnight."

"Ah, but she *didn't* come out of nowhere. It's more that she's part of the community, someone with no prospects of improving her life, and it all snaps one night. She decides to make a difference, to be remembered for something. I'm guessing it snowballed from there, driven by the city's reaction to her. The problem here isn't the girl in the costume, it's the symbol she has become."

"That's why you didn't just kill her when she showed up?" He'd been right. The guy wasn't actually insane at all.

"I never wanted to kill her." Eyes intense, Chaos leaned in towards the mayor. "If you kill her, she becomes a martyr for people to rally around. A symbol for rising up against the oppressors. In this case, that would be you and your group. The only way of dealing with this in a way that will calm down the people is to discredit the Sting. Make them believe that she is actually a danger to them. That her antics are not going to change anything, and may even lead to folks dying."

The mayor nodded. It made sense. "You come in as Mister Chaos, and show the city that her very existence is what put them in harm's way. When she fails to save them, they stop seeing her as a symbol of hope, and things can get back to normal."

Chaos smiled. "And *then* we kill her."

There was another double knock on the glass window. Chaos grabbed his mask and pulled it back on. The mayor gestured to the masked man to stay where he was, and went into the observation room, where he found that Spanky had joined Wade.

"I told you the guy was good," Spanky said, toothpick clenched in his teeth. "He sees the big picture."

"He's over-thinking it if you ask me." Furlong leaned back against the wall. "It doesn't need to be this complicated. Fuck the psychobabble. Kill the Sting and this is done."

"Is it?" Rock shook his head. "Two days ago, you were calling her 'that crazy bitch', but now you're using the name she gave herself. Look at her from the outside, and she's taken out a meth lab, stopped a bank robbery, stopped a drive-by shooter, and then defused a lethal hostage situation with no further casualties after she got on the scene. She's on the verge of being a folk hero. People want someone to believe in, and they've found it. We've done nothing but help that. Everything since the meth lab is on us. We gave her the opportunities because of how we reacted."

"Give Mister Chaos the chance to finish the job," Spanky said to Furlong. "He'll get it sorted, and then we can get back to our plan. Hell, if he does it right it might even make our plan easier."

Wade threw his hands up in defeat. "Fine. Give him another chance."

Rock went back into the interrogation room and took his seat again. "What do you need from me to finish this?"

Chaos left his mask on this time. "Most of the time it comes down to 'us against them.' It's time you became part of the 'us.' The Sting captured a cop-killer. You should show your appreciation for the city's superhero, and hold a celebration."

"You're serious?" The mayor stared at him for a long moment. "You want me to throw a party for a vigilante? Hell, maybe I should throw in the key to the city while I'm at it?"

"That would be a great touch." Chaos smiled. "Get the people to see you on *their* side, instead of as the symbol of what's wrong with Blythe. Get her to come out into the open a bit more. When she does, I'll bring down a massacre so epic that it will be the lead on every news network around the world. Hell, invite the networks for the ceremony. We'll make this city the most dangerous place in the world."

Rock though about what a massacre like that would do to the city. People would be terrified. They'd move out in droves. Travelers would avoid the place as if their life depended on it, because it did. Property values would tank overnight. Local commerce would collapse. Shops and businesses would be forced into bankruptcy. Downtown would be a sea of boarded-up windows. The city's financial situation was already desperate, but this would push it into a truly cataclysmic spiral. The fallout would give Blythe a truly international reputation for disaster.

It occurred to him just how appropriate the name 'Mister Chaos' was.

The mayor smiled a slow and terrible smile. "It's *perfect*. I'll set it up."

Chaos nodded. "How long will you need?"

"A couple days." Rock checked the calendar on his phone. "We could do this on Saturday night. You'll have to stay in jail until then."

"That's fine. Just have the detective keep the orange sodas and Nutter Butters coming."

The mayor paused. "About that. The soda and cookies—is that part of the crazy act?"

"Nope." Chaos laughed. "It's just what I like to eat."

The mayor returned to his car, fighting the urge to chuckle. He needed to make a list of things for the celebration and get Audrey working on it right away. He'd have to put in rush orders on a key to the city and to get banners made in time. Some local businesses might want to get involved. Make it look as official as possible. Maybe one of the gun shops would gift her some fancy bullets or something. Louie Louie's could name a burger after her. Hey! He could ask the high school band to play. If some teenagers got wiped out, it would make the news story absolutely irresistible. Constant prime-time.

Since the Sting had showed up, he'd been worrying that she would be the undoing of all of his plans. That she would ruin everything. But Chaos had shown him the truth. She was a blessing in gold and black armor, the final piece of the puzzle.

And like the masked man had said, once she had made him insanely rich, they still got to kill her.

CHAPTER FIFTEEN

The first thing Erin did on waking was to throw herself into the shower. She was surprised to find remarkably strong water pressure and an almost brand-new showerhead with massage settings. That kept her in there about twenty minutes longer than she'd figured for, but the pulsating water and heat did wonders for her aching muscles. She'd been pushing herself in ways that she hadn't since the service, and her body just wasn't used to it anymore. The longer she stood under the hot water, the better she felt.

Once out and dried off, she put on a pair of jeans and her interview blouse. Bernie hadn't been dressed up when she'd gone by as the Sting, so she gambled that it would be okay. She finished getting ready and headed out, fingers crossed that he'd understand why she hadn't shown up yesterday. She didn't have much money left, but the shower had eaten up a lot of time, so she called up an Uber. Fifteen minutes later she stood at the front door of the Blythe Bulletin.

She knocked and heard a muffled "Come in!"

Bernie was packing a few things into a satchel, and took a minute before looking up. "I'll be with you in just a second... Oh my god, you're here!" He smiled widely and stuck out his hand. "Does this mean you're taking the job?"

"If you'll still have me. I'm sorry I didn't turn up yesterday." She shook his hand.

"Don't worry about it." He glanced around the room at the unmade second desk. "I meant to build that for you, but things got a little interesting yesterday."

"I saw. I'm glad you're okay."

"Me too." He chuckled. "It was pretty surreal, I have to admit. But anyway, I have to drive out to L.A. in hopes of asking someone some questions. I'm not set up for you yet. So you can either start tomorrow, or go with me to L.A.?"

Erin had been waiting so long to get her life back on track that the idea of delaying it another day sent a streak of panic through her. "No! I'll go with you!"

"Great. I can catch you up on the way." He threw the satchel over his shoulder. "Let's go."

Bernie drove along Interstate 10 at a speed comfortably above the limit. He'd handed Erin his satchel when they'd gotten in and had her pull out the envelope he'd received the day before. While he put in a CD—some band called the Winery Dogs, set low enough to talk over—she took a look at the heavily redacted letter it contained. She tried to make sense out of what little was there. There really wasn't much to go on. References to a proposal called Project: Camelot, and a half-dozen cities, all in California, including Blythe.

"This has us driving to Los Angeles?" she asked.

"Well, that and a phone call I made to an old friend who works up in Sacramento. She wouldn't say much. Okay, she said almost nothing at all. But she did tell me that Project: Camelot has something to do with Quentin West."

Her eyes widened. "The billionaire guy who's constantly talking about trying to save the planet? That's not who we're going to go meet, is it?"

"No, we're not meeting West." Bernie shook his head. "That would mean he was expecting us. We're going to *ambush* him, after a presentation at a tech conference this morning."

Her eyes got even bigger. "And you think he'll just stop and talk about his top-secret project?"

"Yes, I do." He turned and grinned at her. "I've got a plan."

"Tell me it doesn't involve kidnapping, drugs or nudity, or you can pull over and let me out right now."

"No, nothing like that." He sounded a little hurt, and turned back to the road. "People like West are proud of their ideas and creations. If this is truly his project, he probably really wants to talk about it. I'm just going to try and provide him the opportunity. Why would you think it would involve any of those things?"

"They're the only scenarios I can think of where we get him to talk with relative certainty," she admitted. "Military training dies hard."

"So it seems." After a beat he turned his head back to her. "In your scenario, who is naked?"

She arched her eyebrows at him. "Is that really a proper work-related question on a girl's first day on the job? Do we have an HR department?"

Bernie turn a little red and focused on his driving.

She stifled a laugh. *This job just might turn out to be fun.*

The trip to L.A. took about three hours, putting them at the downtown Crown West hotel a little after noon. West owned the place, which is why he'd hosted the conference there—he didn't stray far from his own properties. According to online sources, he was creature of habit. He kept a strict schedule, and liked to work out in the afternoons, right after eating. Bernie figured that he'd be in the hotel gym around twelve thirty, so they parked the car and headed straight there.

West hadn't taken over the whole gym or anything, but he did have two security people standing nearby as he jogged on a treadmill. There were a few other people working out in the place, but all of them stayed well away.

Erin thought that maybe they should grab some work-out gear and try to blend in, but Bernie's research had said that West ran for exactly thirty minutes, so stealth was out. She decided to be quiet and watch her new boss in action, learn from his experience.

He walked straight towards the billionaire, and was immediately blocked by a mountain of a man who stopped him a good ten feet from his target. "Mr. West! I'm Bernie Green, Blythe Bulletin, and I have a few questions about one of your projects. If I could—"

A hand the size of a Christmas ham thumped into Bernie's chest and pushed him back three feet. Erin had to side-step to avoid being slammed into.

"Mr. West! Please! I only need a few minutes of your time!"

The hand pushed again, this time sending Bernie back another six feet. The mountain closed the gap while his colleague, another mountain, slid over behind him. They were good at their job, for sure. West never even turned to acknowledge he was being talked to.

"Mr. West!"

The third push sent the reporter up against the gym door, and it looked like the bodyguard meant to put him on the other side of it.

Erin decided it was time to go all in. "Camelot!" she called.

West turned quickly, stumbling mid-stride, but he caught himself and hopped off the machine. "Wait up, Larry."

The first mountain stopped in his tracks, while the second moved over to shut off the treadmill.

West came over to the door and looked directly at Erin. "Why did you say that?"

"Because that's why we're here. Project: Camelot."

He titled his head, but kept eye contact. "What do you know about it?"

"We'll share if you do." She used her best poker face to conceal the fact that other than the name, they had nothing else to share.

He looked over at Bernie. "Where did you say you were from again?"

"The Blythe Banner."

"Fine." He turned and walked towards the locker rooms. "Let's go someplace more private."

Five minutes later, Erin was wearing nothing but a towel, and walking into a sauna with her new boss and one of the richest men in the country. The pet mountains waited outside, to make sure they weren't disturbed.

"Since you're from Blythe, then I guess you know you're one of the candidate cities." He poured some water on the hot coals to get the steam going. "I'd like to know who leaked the information."

"I'm a reporter, and the first thing you ask me is for my source?" Bernie laughed. "We both know your thing is making the world a better place. If Camelot was nefarious, you wouldn't be involved. We're not necessarily looking to blow this wide open. We're just trying to put some pieces together."

West stared at Bernie and Erin through the steam, and bit his bottom lip. He looked torn.

Erin though about it for a moment. Camelot. King Arthur's city of hope. She took another chance. "You're trying to build a new city. Something special..."

"Yes!" West blossomed with sudden enthusiasm. "A city built with all of the latest green technology as part of its founding plan. Integrating all of the advancements from the beginning, instead of trying to wedge it into existing infrastructure like we had to do in Silicon Valley. Set in an open area, where we can put up enough windmills and solar panels to fuel the whole community. Water reclamation centers, recycling plants, clever and human-focused zoning, the latest in agricultural science. We have companies designing ways to grow food on Mars that would work even better here in the desert."

"And you plan to choose one of six existing cities to do this with." Bernie wiped his soaking forehead. "What about the people who already live there? Is this going to be an eminent domain thing where the government just pushes people out?"

West looked offended. "Of course not! The residents will be given two options, either sell their property at slightly above fair market value, or stay and get one of the new modular homes we'll be putting in. The new places might not be as big as the properties they currently have, but they'll be of similar value even before the new city becomes desirable. We're going to improve the quality of life for everyone in the area, regardless of whether they want to stay or leave."

"That sounds a little too good to be true," Erin said. "Why would you choose a place like Blythe to do this in?"

"Cost," West said frankly. "The value of property in California is through the roof, and it's not coming back down. There's a lot of companies that want to be in the state, but can't find a piece of land to build on, not with the infrastructure to make it feasible. Your town is on one of the biggest highways in the nation. With lower property costs, you can bring in self-sustaining electricity and water supplies. These are the types of environment that corporations are looking for to set up their next major manufacturing and distribution centers. We build the city of the future, and it will become the prototype for fixing every economically-challenged place in the country. Cities have always been built around the industries that supported them. We're trying to build an efficient green city that will save the planet *and* its industries."

Bernie sat back, rubbing his chin. "This doesn't make sense. Why would someone want to leak this information to me?"

"What were you told?"

He looked at the billionaire for a moment. "I was given a copy of a letter to the governor that was mostly redacted. All I could see was the names of the cities, the Project: Camelot title, and a few other stray pieces. Nothing that even hinted at anything damning."

"That sounds like the letter I sent to the governor, letting him know the cities we were considering. It's the only thing we've put down on paper. Everything else has been handshakes and promises until we settle the location issue." West shook his head. "I can't even think of a single thing on there that would be worth redacting except the city names."

"It sounds like someone wanted us to think it was suspicious, and start asking questions." Erin adjusted her towel as she moved a little closer. "What were the criteria used to pick the cities, and how will a final location be selected?"

West hesitated again, almost seeming ashamed, but finally spoke. "We realized that we needed to make as big of an economic change as a technological one. We couldn't just make a place slightly better and have any impact. So we looked for the poorest areas of California. The towns where an influx of new jobs and good housing would make the biggest positive impact."

"And receive the least resistance," Erin added. "You basically looked for the shitholes."

West stood. "What will the Blythe Bulletin be saying about this?"

"For now, nothing." Bernie stood as well. "It feels like someone is trying to use us in some way, and I don't particularly like it. At this point, an article about the project would only set up five cities for disappointment."

The billionaire nodded. "I would appreciate a heads up if that is going to change in the future."

"Of course."

West shook their hands and headed out of the sauna, leaving them alone.

Bernie watched the door close. "What's your read on this?"

She frowned. "Someone somewhere is going to try and make a big profit off of this, but I don't quite see how. When we figure that out, everything else should fall into place."

"Sounds about right." Bernie held the sauna door open. "Let's hit a drive-through, and then get back on the road before traffic picks up."

She stopped, and tapped on his bare chest. "You were shocked at my scenarios for getting answers, yet here we are—both naked."

He laughed. "Welcome to the Blythe Bulletin, Erin Cooper."

CHAPTER SIXTEEN

The drive back to Blythe was a somber one. Erin watched the expressions flit across Bernie's face as he wrestled with Project: Camelot. She could imagine what he was thinking—it would be a huge story, but he'd also be setting many of the townsfolk up for a crushing disappointment. Of course, the project might be a lot more sinister than it appeared, in which case keeping it quiet was a betrayal. But if it wasn't sinister, and it really didn't feel like it was, he'd be harming people's interests by getting in the way. Then, of course, there was the anonymous tipster. The Chronicle was being used, but by who, and to what ends?

She waited as long as she could to say it. "You can't run the story. It wouldn't be fair to those struggling to get by."

"You mean everyone. And you're right." He shook his head. "As good a story as this is, it will be just as good when and if the city is picked. Or it will be great for another city. No sense getting people's hopes up for something that might not work out."

She smiled, glad he felt the same way. "But why would someone send you that page?"

"I think it was supposed to get me looking into something else." He turned to her. "I think the question we should be asking is, who could benefit from knowing this information early?"

She sat quiet for a moment. She thought about everything that had happened to her in Blythe recently. The meth lab, the bank robbery, the cops shooting up the trailer park, the wacko trying to kill her. There was one thing all those events had in common. The potential for innocent people to get hurt. "Someone could actively try to drive as many people as possible out of town before the announcement, and buy up the land dirt cheap."

He nodded. "And West wants his project to make the biggest impact possible, so he's going to choose the worst city of the group. The worse Blythe becomes, the better the odds of it being picked."

"Since the cops are doing almost nothing to stop things from getting worse," she added, "it stands to reason that someone in city government is part of the problem."

"Mayor Carrington, the police... There aren't a lot of people to choose from." He sighed loudly. "Exposing the corruption would force the story out into the public anyway—and would a corrupt city government eliminate Blythe as a candidate?"

"What is the right move, then?"

He shook his head sorrowfully. "I honestly don't know."

The rest of the ride home was quiet. By the time they got back to the office, the sun was going down. Bernie asked if she wanted to get dinner or needed a ride home, but she declined both. She didn't know if exposing the project and the corruption was the right move, but it would be a waste of time if they didn't have evidence to back it up.

The *$.99 Is So Fine* discount store was a block from the office. Erin told her new boss she had a few errands to run, and would see him in the morning.

"I grab breakfast most mornings at Phil's across the street." He pointed at the dinner. "If you get in before 9am, you'll find me there."

She wished him a good evening and headed up the street to the discount store. Harsh halogen lights hummed overhead as she made her way to the party supply aisle. The Sting gear wouldn't do. The people looked at the Sting as a hero and she wasn't going to risk tarnishing that.

At the far end of the aisle was a collection of left-over costume pieces from the previous Halloween. She picked up a ninja mask, a flimsy grim reaper costume, and two cans of spray string. She then went to hardware and found a pair of gray work gloves. After that she stopped by the tech section, smirked at the floppy disks, and picked up a small USB drive. Finally she grabbed an energy drink on her way to the register, and for seven dollars was all set for a little breaking and entering.

It didn't take long to walk from the store to city hall, drinking the energy drink along the way. Her plan was simple. The best ones always were. Less that could go wrong. She'd been to city hall to apply for a few different jobs. The thing that always made her laugh was that the door to the mayor's office was next to the restrooms. *You'd think being the head of a city would grant you a bit more distance from the toilets, but not in Blythe.* Or maybe it was considered a perk not having to walk across the building to go.

The building was still open, even though most of the offices were closed. People who worked two or three jobs needing to drop off late utility bills, maybe. She got in without anyone seeing her, and made her way to the bathroom. She gave the stalls a quick check, then locked herself inside one and opened the bag. She wriggled into the grim reaper outfit, put on the ninja mask and the gloves, and tied the bag, which still held the USB and spray string, around her belt.

After another check to make sure the bathroom was still clear, she climbed up onto the toilet and pushed aside one of the squares in the drop ceiling. The tank was enough of a step to get her into the crawlspace on her hands and knees. Her cell phone worked well enough as a flashlight. She put the square of foam back. The crawlspace was about two feet high. She kept her weight on the crossbeams and, praying that they weren't too cheap and shoddy, inched forwards.

After a minor eternity, and about fifteen feet of cobwebby crawling, she shut off her light and slowly lifted one of the squares to peek.

It had to be the mayor's main office—a nice desk, expensive laptop, a great chair, two crappy chairs on the other side of the desk, good carpets, and some bookcases filled with those leather-spined books you bought just to look cultured. No people. The bronzed desk lamp had been left on. She lowered the square and moved herself above where the desk was. She then lifted that square and lowered herself down onto the desk as quietly as she could.

The mayor's chair was just as comfy as it had looked. Erin hit the spacebar on the computer. It immediately came to life showing a lock-screen. She looked around the room, but very little seemed personal. No family photos, no knickknacks or keepsakes. Not even one of those vinyl figures that seemed to be everywhere. Nothing that gave even a hint of what the mayor might use as a password. She quietly started opening drawers. Most of them were filled with documents and sheaves of notes—a surprising number of them for the computer age. She started going through the notes, looking for anything related to Project: Camelot.

She struck out with the first two drawers, but the third one had a folder marked 'West' in the corner. Inside the folder was the same letter that Bernie had received, except this one was not redacted. There were a few other documents in there as well. She took pictures of it all on her cell phone and then put it all back. The last drawer was filled with business cards and restaurant rewards cards, and a single yellow post-it note stuck to the side that read, "Password: Bicycle123".

She typed in the word from the post-it note and the computer opened up. Stifling a grin, she quickly scanned through his files until she found a folder that simply said, "work stuff". There were spreadsheets showing properties he owned and properties he was watching, and several other files that might be of interest. There was also a folder full of rather intimate and revealing images of a young woman who looked very happy to be having her picture taken. She had no idea how that tied into everything else in the folder, but she saved it all to the USB drive just in case.

She got up and pushed the chair back in, and was about to climb up to leave when she heard the office door open. There was a gasp. Turning, she was surprised to see the woman from the photos staring at her with wide eyes. The newcomer let out a short scream, turned, and ran.

Erin grabbed the cans of spray string from their bag, popped off the tops, and began festooning spray string all over the office. As soon as there was a big mess everywhere, she crashed through the door into the outer office and from there into the hallway. Heavy boots were pounding her way. She darted for the emergency exit past the restrooms and hit the door, setting the alarm off as she ran out into the night.

She was across the street and behind a row of cars before anyone came out of the door. Keeping low, she pulled off the mask, gloves and costume. The security guard was barely audible over the sound of the alarm. There was a pick-up truck next to the ford she was crouched behind, its bed temptingly close. She sidled over and shoved her disguise up inside the rim of its spare tire. The spray cans went into a recycling barrel a few feet further away, next to a pharmacy. Feeling more secure, she slid the USB drive into the cup of her bra, just under her left breast. Then she casually stood up and walked across the parking lot to a Donut Shack. She ordered an apple fritter and a cup of coffee, then took a seat by the window to watch the action.

She was on her second donut—a bear claw—and her third cup of coffee when things started to die down across the street. A patrolman made his way over to get a coffee for himself. The kid behind the counter, curious at what was going on, asked the cop about the commotion.

The cop shrugged. "Some punk bust into the mayor's office to vandalize it. The secretary scared them off."

The kid smirked. "Huh."

Erin jumped into the conversation. "It was a political statement?"

"Might have been." The cop chuckled. "They never got to leave a message or anything, just a mess."

She smiled at the officer. "Any idea who did it?"

"A skinny kid in black, one with an ax to grind I guess. You didn't see anyone come out, did ya?"

Erin and the donut server both shook their heads.

"Of course not. It could be half the high school." He shook his head. "Have a safe evening, folks."

She watched the officer leave, then pulled out her cell phone. The photos of the documents from the mayor's desk covered the same information that she and Bernie had gotten from West earlier that day. There really was nothing worth redacting, unless you wanted to set Bernie on the trail to West in search of answers. It seemed like a stretch though. Why would someone want them to go talk to West?

A headache was starting to form behind her eyes, and she rubbed at them. This whole thing felt like being forced to play chess without getting to see the board. How did the secretary play into it? A guy having a fling with his secretary was no big thing, nor was having nude photos on your computer, but why'd he keep them in the same folder as his property listings?

She was done trying to figure it out for the evening. Maybe she'd show it all to Bernie tomorrow and see what he thought. Or maybe not. She wasn't sure how he'd react to her breaking in and swiping the information. She had been so focused on trying to find out what was going on that she hadn't even thought about what to do with the information once she had it. Something else to figure out in the morning.

There was only a short wait for a bus towards home. She hopped off on the corner by the gas station, where she picked up a six-pack of beer and a bag of chips. Then she walked the short distance to her trailer, where she quickly changed into a pair of sweats and a t-shirt before curling up on the couch, popping open a beer and turning on the TV. Flipping through the channels, she settled on a cooking competition show where the chefs were given baskets of strange foods and challenged to make a meal out of them.

Erin liked the concept of cooking. Of knowing food and spices so well that you could just look at a basket of stray items and know how to prepare each of them, make all the flavors work together without having to look anything up. It was more than an art form, it was like magic. She had no idea how to do any of it. Given a can or a box with instructions on the back, she could follow them perfectly. But taking four or five different foodstuffs and fitting them all together harmoniously from nothing, that was brilliance.

Robert had tried to show her how to cook. He told her that you learned from experience, that cooking was experimenting to find what worked together. One item complimented the flavor of another, then you added a third which worked with the combination, and so on until you had the meal you wanted. You just had to know what things mixed well with each other.

That was when it hit her. The mayor wasn't the chef. He was just one of the ingredients in the box called Blythe. Someone else was mixing and matching things to get exactly what they wanted. Someone was pulling his strings, just as they had pulled Bernie's to send him to meet West. Someone out there was the master chef.

CHAPTER SEVENTEEN

Morning came quickly, and Erin was up and ready to go by seven. She swung by Mr. Johnson's trailer to say hello, and to ask him for an envelope. The old man seemed happy to see her, and after looking out an envelope for her, told her that he had something to show her. He led her to the hole in the fence that led to the storage facility, and stepped through.

"You knew this was here?" she asked.

"Who do you think cut it?" He chuckled. "This saves me ten minutes every time I need to come over here. I'm old. I don't have the time or energy to waste."

They made their way to a corner unit at the very back of the facility. He didn't walk to the roll up door though, but stepped around a stack of pallets to the side. She followed him and found a door that was completely hidden from view. He put his thumb against the lock and there was a loud click.

"It's keyed to both of our thumbprints, either hand." He opened the door and stepped back, so she could go inside.

As she entered, the lights came on. Her jaw dropped. She'd been expecting the usual dingy-looking cubicle room filled with dirty boxes and unused exercise equipment. This was a high-tech headquarters that any vigilante would kill for. A workstation boasted one of the largest computer screens she'd ever seen. Racks full of ammunition sat below a variety of weapons. Next to these were a grappling-hook gun and some kind of metal shield. A set of brackets on one wall looked like a station to hold her armor ready for a moment's notice. There were cabinets with a ton of drawers whose contents she couldn't even guess at. It was a genuine secret base, wedged into a ten-foot by twenty-foot storage unit. But the thing that got her attention the most was the black and gold motorcycle.

He tapped the tank on the bike. "Figured we can't have you running from place to place, and no hero should show up in a Ford Focus."

"This looks amazing." She circled around the motorcycle, taking it in.

"Don't be too impressed, it's not new." He walked over and took a seat on the stool at the work station. "It's a 2006 Yamaha YZF-R1. One of my renters was way behind, and offered it to me to help him catch up. Figured I could clean it up, put a little work in, add a few extra bells and whistles that might help the Sting."

He pressed a button on the handle and a sliding door in the back of the unit slid open. It was smaller than the roll up door, and almost silent. It was just big enough for the bike to fit through, and led into what looked to be an alley. Erin stepped through the door and noticed that there was a cinderblock wall about four feet behind the storage unit.

"You come out of the unit and head down this alley, and it lets you out onto the road. It should cover your entrances and exits. There's an alcove about halfway down with a sliding door in case you're being followed. It's triggered by the same button."

"I'm blown away, seriously." She went back into the unit. "But, this is a crazy amount of time, effort and money to put into something you had no idea I'd even go along with. Why?"

"Because I saw somebody in this city step up to do the right thing, and I wanted to give them the chance to do it again." He shut the sliding door. "Besides, I'm old. I have a lot of free time and I can only watch so many re-runs of NCIS. It felt good to have a project again."

"Well, I appreciate what you've done. It's incredible. But I'll have to get the tutorial on the bike later. I need to get to the office."

He tossed her a set of keys.

She caught them and looked them over. "Are these for the bike?"

"I put fingerprint and biometric scanners on everything else and you think I'm going to leave the souped-up motorcycle with a keyed ignition?" He tried to look insulted. "There's a light blue Volkswagen Golf in the guest spot by my trailer. You can use it until you can buy a car of your own."

"Wow. Thank you." She walked towards the door then stopped and glanced back at the old man. "You know, if this is some kind of weird fetish thing where you get your kicks by being my sugar daddy while I go out and fight crime in a skin-tight black costume, I'm okay with that. *Never* tell me that's the reason. But I'm okay with it in theory."

He laughed and shook his head. "Go on, get to work. I'm going to stay here for a bit. I have to finish setting up the computer system."

She waved goodbye and headed back to the hole in the fence.

The VW was at least fifteen years old, and it needed some body work, new seats and a paint job. But it ran well and got her where she needed to go, so she was happy. She made it to the office about quarter after eight. Bernie's car was there, but the door was still locked. She remembered what he said about breakfast, and jogged across the street. Phil's diner was a good-sized restaurant. It had once been part of a national chain that specialized in pancakes. In fact, it looked like it still was, except for the generic sign that said *Phil's*. The place was about half-full, and the average age of the customers had to fall into senior discount territory.

Bernie was in a booth along the side, with his back to her. A waitress was at his table, taking his order. She had a weak smile on her face that wasn't convincing anyone. Erin made her way over to them.

"Morning boss, mind if I join you?"

Bernie turned and smiled at her. "Please do."

She slid into the booth on the opposite side. A small laminated sign on the table said *Breakfast Special*. She looked up at the waitress. "Can I get the special? With, uh, the pancakes, eggs scrambled well, bacon on the rubbery side, and coffee."

The waitress nodded, not writing any of it down, and glided off into the back. A moment later she was back with a cup of coffee, and then vanished again like she'd never been there.   "She's fast," Erin said.

"Yes, she is. The food comes out almost as quickly." He slid the dish of creamers over to her. "I'm glad you decided to join me. Thought maybe you'd had enough of me in the car ride yesterday."

"I've got a lot to learn with this job, so the more time with the teacher the better." She pulled the envelope out of her pocket. "And I figured you'd want to see this. It was on your car window when I got to the office."

He took the envelope and opened it up. Inside was the USB drive, and a note that read, *Courtesy of Mayor Carrington – The Sting.* His eyes went wide and he dug into his satchel, pulling out a laptop. "I've only been here a few minutes. She must have stopped by as soon as I walked across the street."

Erin sat quietly while he booted up, trying to look innocently curious.

He leaned forward and lowered his voice, so only she could hear him. "I got a report that someone broke into the Mayor's office last night and vandalized it. I bet it was the Sting, and she just messed up the office to cover her tracks."

"You think so?" she whispered back.

"She seems to be really clever." He glanced around the diner then back to Erin. "You don't think this has to do with Camelot?"

She pointed at the computer. "Only one way to find out."

"Oh, right." He slipped the drive into a USB port and started typing.

She couldn't see the screen, and kept her mouth shut so she didn't accidentally give away any knowledge of the contents.

He kept typing and clicking on things. "There's a lot of spreadsheets in here. I can't say for sure what they're for, but they seem to focus on land ownership in the city. Seems like a lot of it is owned by a handful of people, and the Mayor is one of them. Let's see what's in this folder."

Bernie clicked on something, his face turned as red as the ketchup bottle. He pushed the top of his laptop down so no one could see the screen.

"What is it?"

He glanced around again, trying to tell if anyone had seen anything. Then he leaned back in. "There are nude photos of the Mayor's secretary!"

She did her best not to laugh, but she couldn't resist playing with him a little. "How does she look? Is she sexy? Do you find her hot?"

"She looks... I mean... She's an attractive woman... but not my type." He stammered out.

"Oh, you don't like women?" she asked innocently. "That's cool. I didn't know." She sipped at her coffee.

"I like women," he replied, too quickly. "I just wasn't expecting to see Audrey like that."

"It's Audrey now? You two are on first name basis?"

Before he could reply, the waitress came swooping in to his rescue. She spread all the plates out on the table, refilled both coffee cups and even tossed out a "Let me know if you need anything else," before Erin had time to look at her food. But there were no problems. Her eggs were scrambled well, her bacon was soft, there was a chunk of hash brown with a nice, crisp edge, and two fluffy-looking pancakes on their own plate to the side. Bernie had ordered the special as well, but his eggs were over-easy, he had sausage links instead of bacon, and he'd chosen wheat toast instead of pancakes. She decided not to hold his breakfast choices against him.

While she was checking out the food, he shut off the laptop, removed the USB drive and dropped it into his shirt pocket, and placed the laptop back in his bag so he could focus on breakfast. "We'll look at that closer back at the office."

"You mean Audrey? I bet you will." She smiled.

He put his forehead in his palm and sighed. "You're just messing with me, aren't you?"

"Absolutely. And you're adorable when you're flustered."

They started in on their food. It wasn't the best meal she'd ever had, but it was hearty, and a hell of a deal at the price—the type of food her father had used to make her before school, back when he worked swing-shift and that was their daily meal together. Her dad hadn't been a great cook, but breakfast was something he made sure did well.

As they were eating, an older woman came up to the table, maybe on the north side of eighty. She approached quietly and put her hand on Bernie's shoulder.

He smiled up at her. "Good morning, Phil."

She had a soft voice with just a hint of an Irish accent. "Morning, lad. You bring a new person into my place without introducing me? I know you were raised better than that."

"I'm sorry." He gestured across the table. "Phil, this is my new co-worker, Erin. Erin, this is Phil, the owner of this fine establishment."

"A pleasure to meet you, lass. You are a beautiful young thing, aren't you?" She looked back to Bernie. "I thought for a moment the boy here had found himself a date."

Erin realized she wasn't the only one who liked to tease her new boss. "It's nice to meet you too."

"I've been reading your bloggy thing, and I wanted to talk to you about the superhero." Phil sat down on the seat next to Bernie, making him slide in a little. "Between you and I, you're not just making this all up, are you?"

"No ma'am. She's very real. Just ask the folks at the bank."

"I don't trust banks or anyone that works for them. But you say she's real, then she's real. I've been in this city a very long time. I've seen it in the good times and way too many bad times. I know what the people are thinking because they come in here and talk about it every morning. And what people are talking about right now is her, the one with the mask."

Erin couldn't help herself. "What are they saying?"

The old woman grinned. "What do you think? They're all amazed that someone is standing up for them. That someone seems to care. Instead of complaining about their bills, or politics or whatever else is weighing them down, they're talking about her. About how she has been saving lives. How she fought the crazy guy with the coat. There's a little girl that comes in here once a week with her grandparents and they bring stuff for her to draw to pass the time. She always draws cats and horses, except this morning."

The woman reached into her pocket and pulled out a folded piece of paper on put it on the table. Bernie took it from her and opened it up, then laid it flat so everyone could see. It was a young child's drawing of a woman with a black mask, gold goggles and short blond hair.

"I told her I liked her drawing and mentioned that you ate here some mornings. She got very excited and asked me to give this to you, so you could give it to the Sting." Phil got back to her feet. "I don't know where that woman came from or why she'd doing what she's doing. But there are a lot of people behind her, and at least one very sweet young girl."

As the older woman walked away, Erin picked up the drawing and took a closer look. The girl had even drawn the escrima sticks on her back. It wasn't perfect—the girl had some talent, but she was young. At that moment though, it was the most beautiful drawing she'd ever seen.

She handed it back to Bernie, who folded it up and slipped it into his coat pocket. They put conversation aside and focused on their breakfasts while the food was warm. With a little start of surprise, she realized that she felt good. The best she'd felt in a very long time. She was hungry, too. She scarfed down everything on her side of the table, including the two pancakes, and nabbed one of the sausages off of his plate when he was done. As they paid the bill and headed back to the office, she felt like it was going to be a very good day.

CHAPTER EIGHTEEN

When they got back to the office, Erin looked over at the still unassembled desk in the corner and wondered if that was where she should begin. Until it was built, she'd be sitting in the chair across the desk from her new boss while he worked. But Bernie took his usual position and gestured for her to sit opposite him.

"Let's see what this will tell us." He pulled the USB drive from his pocket and slotted it into his laptop. No sooner had he pressed the power button then they were startled by an extremely loud sound siren from outside. He whipped the USB back out again. "Damn. Take this."

He handed her the drive, then went for the door. Turning, she saw red and blue lights shining off the wall. She slid the drive into her bra, tucking it into the cup under her left breast. As she was getting her hand back out of her shirt, an officer walked in and wordlessly pushed Bernie towards the wall. She stood, and got as far back as she could. Another officer entered, followed by Detective Furlong, who was holding up a white piece of paper.

"I have a warrant to search the premises," the detective growled. "Stop what you are doing immediately."

"What the hell are you up to, Wade?" Bernie asked, from against the wall.

"You have been in contact with the criminal known as the Sting and we are looking for information pertaining to her identity and whereabouts." He pushed passed his officers, going straight for the laptop. "I'll be taking possession of this."

"You can't do that." Bernie's voice was icy with fury. "This is against the first amendment. I want to see that warrant."

"Look all you want." He pushed the paper into Bernie's chest then turned toward Erin. "And who are you?"

"I'm just here to tell him a story. Can I go?" She tried to look scared, which wasn't too difficult.

"What story?"

"Carl Roets, the guy who retrieves the shopping carts for the local stores… I think he's paying high school kids to take the carts in the first place." She leaned forward like she was telling a secret. "I saw him talking to some kids about a week back, and then just yesterday I saw those same kids riding carts away from the MoreFoods over on Main St."

The detective stared at her. "Why would he care?"

"Carl gets paid by the cart. The more he brings back, the more…"

"I don't mean Carl!" He barked. "Why would Bernie care about that nonsense?"

Erin pulled a shocked expression. "It's illegal! I mean, that's basically stealing from the companies he does business with. I'm surprised you don't know that, Officer."

"Detective," Furlong snapped.

"Really? I would *definitely* have thought you would've known that then, being a detective."

Furlong's eyes narrowed into a scowl. "Go stand in that corner, and do not move or speak until I tell you to."

She quickly moved over to the corner she'd been directed to, and stayed quiet. If he thought she was just a busybody, hopefully he wouldn't bother searching her. She looked over to Bernie. He looked up and made eye contact, then looked down, then made eye contact again and looked down again, over and over. Was he having a seizure? She followed his gaze, and on top of the short bookcase next to her, noticed an envelope—the one that had held the redacted page about Project: Camelot.

She checked out the officers. Furlong had loaded up one of them with the laptop and some papers from the desk, and sent the man out to the car while he pored through the desk's draws. The other was riffling through a file cabinet, dumping documents into boxes. No-one was looking. She slid the envelope across the top of the bookcase and dropped it down the back. Neither of the cops reacted.

Bernie pulled his cell phone from his pocket. "I'm calling my lawyer. This is a clear violation of freedom of the press."

"You're not the press." Furlong grabbed the phone from his hand. "You're just a punk kid writing an internet blog. You have no credentials. You don't even have a print version of your work."

"Give me back my phone." Bernie took a step forward.

Furlong put an arm across his chest and pushed him back against the wall. "Now, you're not trying to interfere with an officer doing his work, are you? Because you can be arrested for that. My warrant gives me the right to take anything related to your business to help aid in our pursuit of the masked criminal. You use this phone as your main business line. It's coming with me."

"Why do you keep calling the Sting a criminal?" Erin asked from the corner.

"Because that's what she is. Her first action was to cause an explosion in a populated trailer park, putting hundreds of people at risk and doing a ton of property damage."

"You mean the meth lab that the cops just ignored?" She stared at the detective. "If you had done your job, Detective, that wouldn't have been an issue."

Furlong pulled away from Bernie and turned toward her as the second officer returned. "If it was a meth lab, any evidence of that fact was blown up. It could easily have been her personal bomb laboratory. On top of that, she has repeatedly put people in harm's way, and we have clear footage of her committing assault—footage we got from Mr. Greene here."

"You're talking about that nut job Chaos, aren't you?"

"She came charging at him with two sticks."

"He'd murdered people and was holding hostages!"

"All the more reason she should've left it to the police. She put everyone there at risk, just so she could be the hero. For all we know, they were working together." He held up the phone. "Which is exactly why the judge let us have the search warrant."

The pressure was building inside her, making her veins throb. Was this idiot really suggesting that she was working with Mr. Chaos? Doing all of this on purpose? Her hands balled into fists, and she took a step towards him.

Bernie lurched away from the wall, putting himself between her and the detective. "Your warrant has nothing to do with Miss Cooper, Detective. Can she leave?"

Furlong glanced around the room. "I think we have everything we need for now. Feel free to go back to work. You can't let that dastardly trolley jockey get away with his cart scam."

The officers picked up boxes of files and headed out, with the detective right behind them. Bernie stayed where he was until they heard the cars pull away, then he moved over and sat behind his desk and sighed. Erin dropped into the chair opposite him, still trying to fight off the urge to punch someone.

"You *can't* let Furlong get you worked up like that." He leaned back in his chair. "The guy is an asshole looking for a fight."

"Did he really think you'd have the Sting's name and number scrawled down on a piece of paper?" She suddenly wanted a beer, badly. But it was far too early, and she was at work.

"No. He came here to deliver a message, most likely for Mayor Carrington."

She leaned forward. "What would that be?"

He smiled and got up from his chair. "To stop writing stories about her. Stop making her look like a hero."

He walked over and leaned his head out the door. He then closed the door, walked over to the short bookcase and pulled it away from the wall. To her surprise, there was a big hole in the plasterboard. He retrieved the envelope she'd dropped, and pulled a plastic bag out from the hole. He tucked the bag under his arm and slid the bookcase back into place. He opened the bag as he came back, pulling out another laptop and placing it on the desk, followed by another phone.

Erin nodded, impressed. "You had a backup ready to go?"

"I'd be stupid not to." He booted up the machine. "It's not hard to see that Carrington is corrupt and only in it for himself. Furlong has to be on the take as well for the mayor to get away with as much as he does. I figured eventually they'd raid this place. Every few days I back up everything to this machine. Last night was the most recent."

"Will they find anything on the one they took?"

"Not likely." He started typing away. "I have the hard drive partitioned into two. It boots up to a system that has just older files and information on it, more than enough to look convincing. But anything new I'm working on is done on the second partition, and that's encrypted and password protected."

"That's very good thinking." She reached into her bra and retrieved the drive. "I assume you want this."

He took the USB and plugged it in. A few key strokes later, the spreadsheet was up. She took her chair around to his side of the desk so she could see. The sheet was broken into a handful of sections, with the name of a Greek god at the top of each section. Under that was a list of addresses and dollar amounts. The gods listed were Zeus, Apollo, Ares, Hephaestus, Poseidon and Dionysus.

"You said that the Mayor was on the list, but I don't see his name." Erin leaned in closer. "How can you tell?"

He pointed at an address under the Zeus heading. "That's the house he uses to have his affair."

"What? You mean with Audrey?"

He opened the other folder, and brought up a picture of the Mayor's secretary lying naked in front of a fireplace. "See the white brick-work on the fireplace? I grew up playing Dungeons & Dragons in front of that fireplace. That was my friend's home. He escaped, and kept the place as a rental for a few years, but he ended up selling it to Carrington last year when the property tax on it suddenly shot up."

There was a knock on the door. Bernie shut the laptop quickly, and tucked it inside the top desk drawer. Erin waited for him to get it put away then opened the door.

The Mayor's secretary breezed in.

At the site of her, Bernie's face turned red again, and he jumped to his feet. "Miss Winters, what a surprise," he stuttered out. "Please come in."

Audrey gave Erin the once-over, then turned her attention to Bernie with a shy smile. "I tried to call, but you weren't picking up and Mayor Carrington wanted you to have this information right away."

"Have a seat." He gestured at the one remaining chair on the other side of his desk. "What can I do for you?"

She sat and politely straightened out her skirt, leaning forward a bit as Bernie was sitting back down. Then she glanced back up at Erin. "Who's this?"

"My apologies." He gestured between the two women. "Audrey Winters, this is my new reporter, Erin Cooper."

"A pleasure to meet you." Erin nodded.

Audrey nodded back, and fished a piece of paper out of her purse and handed it to Bernie. "The Mayor has decided to throw a Thank You Celebration for the Sting."

"What?" Erin blurted out. "Are you kidding?"

"Of course not. It's all on the paper." She kept focused on Bernie. "The Sting stopped a cop killer, and has saved quite a few residents of this city. The people think she's a hero, and the Mayor agrees. He wants to have a ceremony on Saturday where he gives her a key to the city. Hopefully, if you are willing to run the story, she'll get word and show up."

"I would normally have no problem with this." He put the paper down. "But Detective Furlong was just here at the office, confiscating my computer and documents, all to hunt for information on the very person you say the Mayor thinks is a hero. The detective insists she's a criminal and he's going to arrest her. I want no part of an entrapment."

Audrey shook her head. "Wade is jealous. She's done more in just a few weeks than he's done in his entire career on the force. If you look on the paper, you'll see that Mayor Carrington has guaranteed that she will not be arrested or detained in any way, nor will anyone try to discover her identity. This city is alive again. People have hope, and the Mayor sees that, and he knows the Sting is the main reason for it."

"That would be easier to believe if I had my equipment and records back." Bernie picked the paper up again. He started reading over the document.

Erin kept her eye on Audrey. She wasn't sure why, but she really didn't trust the woman. There was more to her than she showed.

He sighed. "You can tell the Mayor I'll *try* to get the story up later today. It would be a lot easier if the police hadn't confiscated everything."

Audrey smiled and got to her feet. "Thank you, Bernie. I'm sure he'll feel like he owes you one. I'll let myself out."

Once she was gone, Erin moved her chair back around the desk and took a seat opposite her boss. He was still reading over the paper and shaking his head.

"This has to be a trap." He slid the paper across to her. "I wouldn't trust Carrington or his promise as far as I could throw him. I shouldn't run it."

She glanced over the paper. "Yes, you should. We got raided this morning because the Sting has come to you already. If you don't run the story, you're telling the Mayor and his cronies that you're on to them. I'm sure she will see this for a trap and stay as far away from it as possible."

"I hope you're right."

She handed him back the paper. "And we really have to work on your poker face. You totally looked like you'd been caught looking at porn when she came in."

CHAPTER NINETEEN

Rock had always been honest with himself. He'd gotten into politics for the power and the money, and he wasn't too worried about rules. Hell, the idea of not only bending the rules but rewriting them had been why politics had attracted him to begin with. His dad used to say that he who made the rules won the game, and Rock had taken that to heart early.

Blythe was a stepping stone. Do the city council for a few years, mayor for a couple of terms, a term or two in the House of Representatives for the area, and then hit the Senate. That was where he was going to stop. Too many eyes on the president. He could sit in the Senate for five or six terms, then retire to the lecture circuit.

The plan had been delayed a little when the previous mayor proved too squeaky clean, and not keen to retire. Spanky had been a great find, more than happy to upload some extremely questionable images to the then-mayor's computer in exchange for some laxity with drug enforcement policies in the area. Rock still remembered the look on the man's face when he was arrested. It had almost made the wait worth it.

Last year, after his two terms as mayor, he was about to announce his run for the House when he got the call from Mr. X. The mysterious caller proved his bona fides rather alarmingly, then told him about Camelot and explained how he could make an absolute ton of money if he hung on a bit. It'd been a dilemma. A ton of money sounded wonderful, but it wasn't power. What had swung him had been realizing that the mayor who helped turn the state's deepest shithole into a thriving metropolis would be a damned good-looking potential senator. Another couple of years in Blythe could catapult him past the House all together.

Then Audrey entered his life. She was alright as a secretary, but far more importantly she was sexy and imaginative, and she didn't care that he was married. She was delighted to see him when he was available, and never pushed for more. Never any talk about him leaving his wife, or their future together. Other than an insatiable appetite and an uncanny ability to distract him at inappropriate times, she was perfect. He set her up in one of the first houses he bought in the area, just a half mile from the office — very convenient for lunch meetings. Soon he was going over there at night more and more too. His wife complained a little, but she was impressed with his dedication to his job.

The sun had already gone down as he pulled into the garage at Audrey's place. It was late enough that he should've just gone home, but arranging the celebration had been a lot of annoying drudgery, and he really needed to unwind. He took off his tie and tossed it onto his briefcase in the passenger seat. He let himself in and went straight for the bar. An Old Fashioned sounded tempting, but thought of all that muddling about with the sugar and orange peel, not to mention finding the damn bitters, drove him into the arms of a bourbon, neat.

Audrey's voice floated down from upstairs. "Is that you, sweetie?"

"Yeah."

"I warmed up the Jacuzzi. I'll be down to join you in a minute."

He wandered outside and saw the bubbles seething on full. He smiled. There was nothing better on a cool night than being in a Jacuzzi with a gorgeous woman.

As if on cue, Audrey walked out of the house carrying two towels and wearing nothing at all. Even after all these months, the sight of her still got him excited. He felt a rush of energy push away his weariness. She placed the towels on a chair, and then sashayed over to kiss him, a short, quick kiss that lingered just long enough to promise more.

"You were working hard today." She started undoing the buttons on his shirt. "I figured a nice, relaxing soak would help those tired bones."

She undid the last button, then left the rest for him and turned to dangle her foot in the water for a second. Her smile let him know the water was perfect, and she stepped in slowly. The water slid over her skin, rising up her thighs, bubbles clinging to the tight curves of her ass as she descended. The water crested just above her hips, and she turned to face him so he could see it lick the bottom of her navel. She reached down and scooped up two handfuls of water, then ladled them over her breasts. Streams cascaded back down into the water off the tips of her nipples.

She glanced up at him. "Are you coming?"

He realized he'd been staring. He put his phone on top of the towels and hurriedly stripped off. A moment later, it was his own foot entering the steaming water. It was hot, a few degrees more than he preferred, but he wasn't going to let that deter him. He took it slowly though, giving his skin a chance to adjust — until he felt her hand wrap around his hardness. She gently pulled him right to her. His skin, already enlivened by the heat, tingled at her silky smoothness as she pressed against him.

She leaned into his ear and whispered, "You don't seem that tired after all."

"You give me energy," he replied, breathlessly.

"Is that what you call it?" She tugged more firmly on him, and he gasped. "Have a seat, and we'll see how much energy you have."

She released him long enough to let him to sit on the front of the bench and lean his shoulders back against the edge. Hot, bubbling waves danced up to the tops of his shoulders and neck. She shimmied in the water, putting on a sensuous show, playing with her breasts until her nipples stood out proud. She turned around, and rubbed herself up and down his chest and stomach while reaching down for him again. Then she tantalizingly lowered herself down onto him, easing him inside her, almost in slow motion. He ached to thrust up to meet her, but knew she wouldn't let him. Once she got fully down, he grabbed her hips, determined to take over.

Which was when his phone rang.

The ring tone — Peter Gabriel's 'Shock the Monkey' — left him no choice but to get it. He reached back to the towels on the chair, and gave them a tug. They fell to the ground, cushioning the phone as it fell with them. He scooped it up and hit answer.

"Did I catch you at a bad time?" asked the familiar computerized voice of Mr. X.

"No. It's fine." His voice wavered as Audrey slid herself up his length, swaying her hips gently. "What can I do for you?"

"Oh, good. I just wanted to ask if you'd gone completely fucking insane?" X sounded surprisingly even-keeled for what he was saying.

"No..." He squirmed as Audrey thrust down hard onto him, enfolding him completely. His head span a little. "What are you referring to?"

"Oh, I don't know. Mr. Chaos, maybe? A celebration to thank the Sting? Are there any other stupid moves I'm missing?"

He grabbed Audrey by the hips and tried to hold her down on him with his free hand. She took it as a sign to roll her hips, squeezing him inside her. He had to bite his lip fiercely to stop his gasp from escaping. "We got, uh, in touch with a consultant about — mmm — our recent insect problem. It was his suggestion, and it... seemed perfectly reasonable."

"Are you talking to me in code?" The mechanical voice was starting to sound irritated. "Insect problem? Who told you to call in a consultant? Who told you to even think?"

He tried to shut out Audrey's soft lips sucking on his earlobe. "I don't appreciate being talked to—"

"Shut up." The voice cracked with anger. "I *specifically* told you to do nothing. I couldn't have made that any clearer. I expected Furlong to try something stupid, because that's what he is. You and Spinello needed to keep him in check. Make this all go away."

He wanted to defend himself, but he had to stay discreet — and Audrey was driving him absolutely insane. It was taking everything he had to stay focused. He smacked her ass sharply to get her attention, but she misinterpreted the spank, and started grinding herself down on him, hot and fierce.

"It's... it's too late to cancel, cancel, ah, the celebration... Tomorrow night."

"I know. But make sure absolutely nothing happens." The voice sounded as stern as any he'd ever heard. "No one tries to arrest the Sting. Hold a nice, quiet ceremony. Give her the key to the city, and let her leave. No-one follows her. Announce that damn pub crawl that you were planning."

He fought down a wild stab of pleasure and pain as Audrey bit his nipple, and took a moment to catch his breath. "Yeah. Sure. I can do that." He took a few more deep breaths, as slow and steady as he could manage. The conversation was almost over.

"Keep Furlong leashed, send Chaos packing, and let the damn city calm down. Understood?"

Audrey slid off of him, making him gasp, and stood up. "Yes. Understood."

The call ended just as she walked up the steps and out of the water. "You could've just told me you weren't in the mood." He could hear the pout in her voice. She wrapped herself in one of the towels, and went into the house.

Rock stared at the closed door and groaned. He needed to go say a few words, and then hopefully they could finish what they'd started. But first he needed to make a call. He activated his phone's third speed dial number.

"Furlong here."

"Wade, it's Rock. I need you to grab Chaos from lockup and send him back to wherever he came from. Our mysterious friend isn't very happy and—"

Furlong interrupted him. "There's a problem with that."

"What?" Rock felt his stomach drop.

"I was just about to call you. Chaos broke out of here, maybe twenty minutes ago. Beat the crap out of two officers, got his gear out of the evidence room, and disappeared." He paused for a second. "I don't remember this being part of the plan."

"That's because it wasn't," the mayor growled. "Put everyone on finding the guy. *Everyone.* Call Spanky and get him to help too — this asshole was *his* idea in the first place."

Rock hung up and tossed the phone back onto the towel. He grabbed his bourbon from the edge of the Jacuzzi and gulped it down in one swallow, then sat back down in the water. Everything was starting to go sideways. They weren't going to find Chaos before the celebration. It would go to hell. And if Mr. X turned on him afterwards, he'd be stuck in the middle of nowhere with a bunch of worthless real estate, and no money to launch a campaign. His plan would die in the desert.

Any thoughts he'd had of finishing things with Audrey were now officially dead.

CHAPTER TWENTY

Erin picked up a pizza and a six pack of beer on the way home that night. The pizza was okay, a bit greasy, but she opened one of the beers and then barely touched it. She was still anxious and jittery after the morning's raid at the office, like she'd started the day with too many shots of espresso. She flipped through the channels on the television, never staying on any station for more than a minute before looking for something better. The longest she stuck with anything was a cooking show where chefs had to try to make a dessert from pomegranates, natto, beer and sauerkraut cake. She wasn't sure what natto was, but it looked disgusting. She couldn't figure out why they would have to make a dessert when they already had cake. It just seemed like a waste of time.

She turned the TV off, put the left-over pizza in the refrigerator and then took a look at a shelf of books the previous owner of the trailer had left. The woman had been a fan of mysteries, and there were books by Agatha Christie, Arthur Conan Doyle, Rex Stout and quite a few others. She selected *Murder on the Orient Express*, a title she'd heard of. She adjusted the side lamp and laid down on the couch, then cracked open the old paperback book and began to read. After a couple of minutes and a few pages, she realized that she had no idea what she'd read, and started over. This happened two more times before she finally gave up on that idea as well.

She wondered if a hot shower might relax her. It was one of the tricks Hertzberg had suggested to try and quell her anger — get in the shower, turn it on hard and hot, and focus on the water hitting her skin. Water pressure in a trailer wasn't great and the hot water ran out quickly, but it was worth a shot. She stripped out of her work clothes and stepped in. First, she busied herself with actually getting clean. Her short hair was always a quick wash. Once she was done with that, she turned her back to the shower head and let the spray hit her between the shoulder blades. It was a bit like a message, but she did like the doc had said, and concentrated on the feel of the water on her skin. She took long, slow breaths, and tried to push the anxiety out of her system in the same way she used to push out the anger.

Fifteen minutes later she was toweled off, and still full of nervous energy. Her last resort was to take a run around the trailer park. It made a bit of mockery of having just showered, but she was out of ideas. She slipped on a pair of dark blue sweats, a khaki colored T-shirt and a pair of white sneakers, then slipped out into the mild night air and began jogging at a decent pace. Her plan was to do a couple laps around the park, hopefully burning off all her energy so she could then get some sleep.

As she made her first pass around the park, she noticed that most of the trailers had their lights off. That didn't really tell her much as a lot of elderly people got to bed really early. But she figured it had to be close to eleven. Even Mr. Johnson had his lights out. As she was finishing the lap, she went by some of the trailers with bullet holes in them. That set her thinking about the two idiots who'd shot up the place, and how one of them had been a cop. And *that* made her think about damned Furlong again. His smug face was filling her mind when she came around on the second lap and took a sharp left through the hole in the fence.

A moment later, she was by the side door of the lair. The name would do until she thought of something better. She went in with no clear idea of what she was going to do, but found herself suiting up anyway. The first time she'd worn the suit, it had felt constrictive. Like there was pressure on every inch of her body at once. For a split second, she'd thought that the old guy had just been being a perv. But the moment the bullets had started flying and she'd sprinted out the door, she'd felt amazing. Better than any uniform she'd ever worn in the Army. Like it was a second skin. Like she was almost invincible.

As she clicked on the belt this time, there was a different feeling. It was relaxing. Like the suit was giving her a warm, protective hug. It was absolutely crazy, but she felt better suited up. The anxiousness was gone. Okay, she was all dressed up with nowhere to go, but that didn't mean she couldn't take the bike out for a spin. It'd be a bad idea if her first time out on it was during an emergency. Yeah. She should definitely take it out. Get used to it. While she was out there, it would probably be a good idea to try out that grappling gun, too. Again, she couldn't afford to be working out the kinks in a moment of need.

It was justification enough. She slipped on her mask, then kicked over the bike and pushed the button for the back door.

The turn out of the back was sharper than she'd expected. Her front tire hit the outer wall, and she had to put her feet down to keep the bike from tipping. Not the best start to an inaugural ride. She got the motorcycle going again, and headed down the long strip behind the units.

To her surprise, even in that confined space, the bike wasn't nearly as loud as she'd expected. She made a mental note to ask the old man how he'd managed that. As she got near the end of the run, a green light lit up in front of her and a door began to open. Above the light, there was an unlit red light — a sensor system maybe, to let her know if anyone was on the other side of the run? Johnson had really thought of everything. She suddenly wondered if there was a *Being A Superhero for Dummies* book with all of this in it. If there wasn't, he needed to write one.

Once on the street, she opened up the throttle to see what the motorcycle could do. It jumped up over a hundred miles per hour in the blink of an eye, and felt like it still had more to give. She didn't keep it there long, though. Too attention-grabbing. She eased back down to a more typical speed, then took it into some side streets, seeing how well it could handle. It felt like it was on a rail, hugging corners and turns effortlessly. She suddenly wished she was up in the mountains, so she could give the bike a real workout.

Thinking of mountains made her realize something. A grappling hook was an odd choice of tools for the area. There were only a handful of buildings in Blythe that were two stories tall, and she couldn't think of a three-story building in the entire city. Where was she going to try it out? She settled on the movie theater. It was a good contender for the tallest building in Blythe. She swung the bike around and headed south.

It only took a few minutes. The parking lot was almost empty. No surprise, for a weeknight well past the final showing. She pulled up along the back of the building and shut the motorcycle off. She glanced around to make sure no one was watching, then retrieved the grappling gun from the little storage area over the rear wheel. The gun was pretty simple in design. It had a barrel where the hook itself went. The prongs folded in, making it look like an eight-inch steel rod. There was a super-thin carbon-fiber line attached to the end. Fixed to the handle of the gun was a flexible tube about two feet long which ended in a disc about the size of a CD and about two inches thick. On the gun itself was an adjustment knob for distance, ten-foot increments up to fifty feet. She glanced up at the roof and figured it was definitely more than twenty, so set it to thirty and fired.

The hook shot out of the gun and the three prongs sprang out into place instantly. The hook cleared the roof and disappeared. She slotted the circular disc into its place on the side of her utility belt, then fastened the gun itself to her belt buckle, as the old man had showed her. She hit the switch on the disc, and for a few seconds nothing happened. Then she was yanked off the ground and pulled quickly up the side of the building. Just a couple of dazed seconds later, she was grabbing onto the edge of the roof and pulling herself over. Once she was sure she was secure, she just laid there, getting her wind back. She'd get better prepared for it next time.

A minute later, she got to her feet. She retrieved the hook, but left it out of the gun for now. Johnson had explained how to use the gun for rappelling as well — secure the hook, slowly let out the line until you got to the ground, then hit the hook return and it would collapse again and reel itself in.

The gun was another really impressive design. How many of these things were his own creation? Or did he just know where to get his hands on them? Not that it mattered. If it hadn't been for the old man, she'd still be running around in paintball gear — or dead, even.

"What are you doing up here?"

The voice startled her. She spun around and had her gun half-out of its holster before she saw a middle-aged man sitting in a folding lawn chair in front of a small, two-man tent. He was working on a laptop that he had sitting on a TV tray in front of him.

"I needed a place to try out my grappling gun," she admitted. "There aren't many tall buildings in the area."

He looked thoughtful for a second. "No, not really. There are the apartments over on Hobsonway and Fifth, but that building is only two stories. I don't think there's going to be a lot of call for a grappling gun around here."

"You're probably right." She took a few steps towards the man. "What are *you* doing up here?"

"I'm Walt Tucker, the assistant manager here at the theater." He gestured towards the building below. "Been here thirteen years now."

"And you sleep on the roof? Is that part of the job description?"

He laughed a little. "No. My girlfriend and I broke up a few months back. She took the apartment. I didn't really have anywhere to go, and the manager told me I couldn't sleep in the building."

"So, you decided to sleep ON the building?"

"Bingo!" He let out a big smile. "I've got a thing for semantics." The smile faltered. "Part of why my girlfriend ended it, probably. Anyway, I'm just staying up here until I can afford first and last on a new place."

"Doesn't it get cold?"

"It's not too bad, really." He gestured to an electrical plug that his laptop was attached to. "I've got a space heater for the bad nights, and I intend to be out of here before the rain comes back."

"Well, you seem to have a solid plan." She was about to set the hook to let herself down, then stopped. "You don't seem surprised at all that I'm up here. Why?"

"You said it yourself — there's not a lot of tall buildings in this city. I've been reading comic books since I was five. The superhero always goes up a tall building and listens for danger. It just made sense that you would end up here sooner or later."

"You think I'm a superhero?" She shook her head. "I've been called a vigilante, a criminal, and a few other things I don't care to repeat. But not a superhero."

"Of course you are. You've got the awesome costume." He held up his hand and started keep track of his points with his fingers. "Your identity is so secret you even use a voice changer. You've already saved multiple people. You've gone up against a costumed villain. The police are after you. You've got impressive gadgets. What else would you be? If I didn't know that the Blythe Bulletin was run by a guy, I'd say you probably masqueraded as a reporter."

She shook her head and laughed, just a little uneasily. "You may have sat through a few too many showings of the summer blockbusters. I'm no hero, super or otherwise."

He threw his hands up in defeat. "Fine. But do you remember the old Batman series with Adam West?"

"Of course."

"Okay, do you remember how he and Robin would climb up the sides of buildings, and sometimes a guest star would pop their head out of a window and have a conversation with them?"

"Vaguely." She thought for a second. "Didn't Jerry Lewis do one of those cameos?"

"Exactly!" He put his hands out wide. "You just climbed up the side of a building. I'm the guest star!"

Erin leaned down and secured the hook to a pipe, then walked towards the edge of the building. "Your girlfriend was an idiot, Walt. She doesn't realize what she's given up."

"Thanks." He chuckled ruefully. "Be careful out there."

She rappelled down the building and retracted the hook. Then she stashed the grappling gun back into its compartment and got back on the bike. She glanced back up at the roof.

A few weeks back, she'd hated Blythe and everyone in it. She'd had to put on a mask to really see who the locals were. Sure, they were a bit crazy, and way too casual about the weird things happening around them, but they were good people. The type of people worth fighting for.

The city was still a shithole, though.

CHAPTER TWENTY-ONE

Bernie parked his car up on Spring and walked the two blocks down to Hobsonway. The celebration was being held in an empty lot on the corner, and from the looks of the crowd in front of him, most of the city had turned out to honor the Sting—or, possibly, to see if she was real. There'd been a time when having the newspaper run a story and show a picture would've been enough, but the divisive nature of the world had made it so people only believed the news they wanted to believe. Everything else just became *Fake News*.

He was surprised at how nice the little event looked. There was a stage thirty feet wide at the back of the lot, with a microphone ready and a blown-up picture of the Sting. A picture *he'd* taken. It hung in front of a set of blue drapes that ran the length of the stage, and matched the bunting that went around the base. Carrington had used that stage in the past for political speeches. Both sides of the lot were lined with vendors under pop-up canopies. You could buy hot dogs, funnel cakes, lemonade, cotton candy and beer. There was a clown to the right of the stage making balloon animals for children, and a pony they could get their picture taken on. The whole thing felt like an impromptu carnival. He could go for a funnel cake.

As he waited in line to buy some deep-fried goodness, he glanced towards the back of the stage and saw the mayor and Furlong talking. Carrington was speaking and waving his arms about. The detective mostly stood still, with his head slightly lowered. It did not appear to be a pleasant conversation from where Bernie was standing. He thought about trying to move closer and listen in, but there really wasn't any kind of cover. With any luck, the reason would become clear later.

He glanced around the lot some more, and noticed something else. There were a lot of people there, but there were also a lot of cops. A lot was a relative term for the small city, but just about every uniformed officer in Blythe appeared to be both on duty and at the celebration. He even spotted a few officers who never got out of the station. One of them, Jim

Lucas, was standing just on the outer edge of the lot, behind the beer vendor. Lucas was about ten years too old to still be on the streets, and about thirty pounds too heavy for his uniform, but there he was, watching the crowd.

Bernie got to the front of the line and ordered two funnel cakes. He then walked over towards Lucas, smiling broadly. "Hey, Jim!"

"Hi, Bernie." The officer smiled back. "Out here covering the big event for the Blythe Bulletin?"

"Absolutely." He held up one of the funnel cakes. "Hey, I accidentally bought two of these. Care to help me out?"

Jim looked down at the treat being held out to him, then glanced around to see if anyone was watching. He was on the opposite side of the stage from the mayor, and out of eye shot of most of the officials. Even so, he checked a second time before taking the funnel cake. After a quick bite, he sighed happily. "Oh, that is so good. The smell has been driving me crazy."

"No kidding." Bernie chomped into his own piece. "I could smell it from two blocks up the street."

They stood for a moment, ate their funnel cakes, and watched the crowd. He wanted the old cop as relaxed as possible. They'd known each other for years, and Lucas was poker buddies with his dad to boot. He was a good source of minor tips for the paper.

"I'm a little surprised to see you tonight," Bernie started, between chews. "I didn't think you worked events anymore."

"I don't." The cop gulped down a bite. "But with the chance the Sting could show up here, and that guy getting loose, they wanted all the eyes on site they could get. Even my nearly blind ones."

Bernie started running that through his head. Someone got loose? Who? And when? Why hadn't the police made an announcement? They usually did. Literally everyone who worked for the department was on site. Who would rate that type of...

He turned towards Jim. "Mr. Chaos *escaped?*"

"Oh shit! I didn't say that, Bernie!" The cop was frantic. "You can't tell anyone I said that."

Bernie glared at his friend. "I protect my sources, Jim. You know that. But a homicidal killer—one who wants to murder the person that this celebration is for—is out on the loose, and that's your first thought? Why the hell is this celebration still going ahead? The mayor should've canceled it. Ordered people into their homes. What the hell is going on?"

"I... Look, I'm not sure. Honest. Furlong told us to be on the watch for him, and to keep quiet."

"Great. Did they at least circulate photos of what he really looks like?" Bernie started nervously scanning the crowd. "Show me and I'll help watch."

Lucas shook his head. "He refused to take his mask off. Claimed it was part of his religion. We were waiting on a judge to make a ruling if we could force him to remove it or not."

"I can't believe this."

Bernie stepped away from the cop and started typing a post for the Blythe Bulletin. He could keep Jim out of it and still damn well try to alert as many people as he could to stay safely away from the event. What the hell were Carrington and Furlong thinking? Did they want to use the ceremony as bait for Chaos? Did they plan to arrest the Sting if she showed up? It couldn't be that they wanted Chaos and Sting to fight again, in the middle of a crowd. That would be absolutely insane. He typed out a short update and hit post without even spell-checking it.

People of Blythe, beware! Unnamed sources have told us that the masked killer, Mr. Chaos, may be on the loose again and could be targeting the celebration event going on this evening. There is a heightened police presence around the ceremony, but as the true identity of Chaos is still unknown, attendance at the celebration could be extremely dangerous. Will update story as more information becomes available...

All he could do was hope the word would spread quickly. His next act had to be to confront the mayor, tell him that the story had been posted, and force him to proactively clear the area before the citizens of the city discovered they were being used for bait. Hopefully that would be a persuasive argument. But as he, turned he realized that the mayor was already on the stage, about to speak. The crowd fell quiet.

"Ladies and Gentlemen, thank you for coming out this evening. As you know, there was a hostage situation a few days ago at the bank, and along with a teller named Gary Wittings, Officer Jeff Lamont was murdered by a man calling himself... Well, his name doesn't matter. What does matters is that Officer Lamont sacrificed himself in a heroic effort to save lives, and I ask you all to join me in a moment of silence in his honor."

The mayor lowered his head, and the crowd followed suit. Bernie glanced around and saw that the officers on duty were keeping their heads up and looking around.

"Thank you." The mayor continued. "There was a second hero that day. One who has just appeared in the last few weeks, and has risked her life multiple times for the people of this city. She headed off a shooting spree in the trailer park, prevented a bank robbery, and took down the man who killed Officer Lamont and Mr. Wittings. As a rule, we don't condone vigilante activity, but she has saved many lives, and shown her love for this city. Tonight, we are here to show that love back to her. Although we don't know her real name, I would like to present this key to the city to the masked hero known as the Sting!"

Carrington held up a two-foot long gold key with a blue ribbon hanging off the end of it. The crowd cheered and applauded. The Palo Verde High School band began to play a version of Scott Joplin's *The Entertainer*. To Bernie's surprise, the crowd started parting to let someone through. He stared as he made out the Sting herself, riding a motorcycle. She drove up to the end of the stage, and leapt up off the bike in a flip, landing on the stage. The cheers and applause turned thunderous. She walked across the stage and shook hands with the beaming mayor, taking the key in her other hand.

Bernie stared at her, aware his jaw was hanging open. He started shooting glances all around the area. There was absolutely no cover up there on the stage. She seemed relaxed, and definitely didn't come over as the type to risk innocent lives. She *had* to be oblivious.

The mayor raised his hands for folks to be quiet, and then gestured for the Sting to speak to the crowd. At that moment, out of the corner of his eye, Bernie saw movement on top of the Fusion Bank building.

He pointed at the roof and screamed, "Get down!"

The crowd has just quieted, and his words carried. She glanced up at the roof, then grabbed the mayor and leapt off the stage into the crowd. A streak of fire raced from the bank building and smashed into the stage. It exploded with a near-deafening blast that rocked him back on his feet. The stage disintegrated into wreckage and shrapnel which—thankfully—flew mostly upwards or away from people. The crowd convulsed and disintegrated into screaming, frenzied fragments. Bernie looked up at the bank to see Chaos holding a rocket launcher. Police officers were starting to turn as well, and several opened fire on him. The killer didn't hesitate. He tossed the launcher aside and leapt off the roof to land on the canopy of the cotton candy stand. The canopy collapsed, but Chaos was already diving forward into the crowd. He rolled once as he landed, and came up in a crouch, with his MK-9 up and ready to fire. It would've been impressive as hell if he hadn't been a homicidal maniac.

The crowd were running in all directions. Bernie kept getting swept back away from the scene, and it was all he could do to keep in earshot. The blast had sent several people in the front row flying. It had also apparently done a number on the mayor and the Sting. Neither of them were on their feet, but at least they appeared to be alive.

Jim Lucas came running in, his standard-issue .38 raised. Before Bernie could yell a warning, Chaos whirled on him and let the bullets fly. The old cop was torn apart by a stream of shots to the chest and stomach. As Bernie fought a wave of horror and nausea, Chaos kept on the trigger.

Five crowd-members behind where Jim had been fell to the ground in a spray of blood.

"Anyone else stupid enough to come at me?" Chaos shouted, and loosed another volley of bullets into the crowd.

The answer came in the form of an escrima stick across the face. The Sting looked shaky, but she was on her feet, and the mayor was leaving the area as quickly as a couple people from the crowd could help him along. Chaos swung his gun towards her, but she smashed him in the wrist with a second stick strike. The gun dropped, and swung back to his side on a strap.

"Aren't you supposed to be in jail?" She stood in a ready stance, sticks raised.

"They ran out of Nutter Butters." He pulled out and then extended his staff. "Besides, how could I miss seeing you get the key to the city? I mean, I'm the reason they like you."

The cops were towards the outer edges of the crowd, waiting for the people to thin out and looking for clear shots. More and more people were running. No-one had been stupid enough to make the same mistake as last time and stay to watch. No-one except Bernie. He couldn't pull himself away.

The Sting circled to the right, putting her back to the stage, so there were fewer people behind her. "We can stand here and banter all day if you like, but you're obviously insane, and I feel like I should try and talk you into getting the help you need."

"Really?" Chaos appeared distracted by the thought. "You think I'm crazy and want to help me?"

"I said that's what I *should* do. What I *want* to do is kick your ass again." She leapt at him, a series of fierce strikes buzzing at his head.

Even Bernie could see that her attacks weren't crisp as they'd been the other day. Was she still groggy from the explosion? Chaos deflected two of the three blows, and simply ducked under the last one. Her move left her midsection open, and he slammed a fist into her stomach. As she doubled over, he drove a knee up into her face. She staggered back, one of her sticks falling from her hand. Chaos took a step forward and swung his staff around, catching her across the knee and then sweeping her legs out from under her. She crashed to the ground hard.

He stood over her, spinning the stick idly across his hand. "I'd hoped this would've been a big final fight for us where I could kill you with a lot of people watching. But you're just not up for a big fight, are you?"

"I'm up to taking you out." The Sting rolled onto her side and tried to get back to her feet.

He swung his staff down with incredible force, catching her on the side of the head with a sickening thud. Her body instantly went limp, and she collapsed in the dirt. He stood over her and laughed.

It was more than Bernie could take. He charged the masked killer, his only plan to do *something*. Tackle the guy and hold him while cops moved in, that could work.

Chaos spun around and backhanded him casually across the face. The world spun, and he landed in the dirt, his cheek a blaze of pain. Before he could even blink, Chaos had that gun pointed squarely between his eyes.

"Have enough people died yet today?" Chaos was calling loudly enough for all the cops to hear. "I'm totally willing to kill some more. But I'm also happy just taking the Sting with me and leaving. So if you want this to end now, put away your weapons."

Furlong was among the officers who'd been trying to move in. "Do what he says. We don't want anyone else hurt."

There was some rustling of leather, and after a moment, Chaos nodded. He walked over to the Sting and picked her up easily. He carried her for a few feet, then stopped and crouched down to pick up the key to the city as well. "For a small town, you guys put on a pretty fun celebration."

Bernie watched as the killer carried her to the bank's parking lot, dumped her inside a black SUV, then got in and drove off. As the SUV vanished, he got painfully to his feet. Blood was pouring from his nose, down over his mouth. Any pain he felt had vanished in the white-hot fury that engulfed him. Jim was dead. Bodies were strewn about the empty lot. And a woman who had done nothing but try to help the city was in the hands of an insane killer.

Everything there had been preventable. The carnage fell squarely on the shoulders of Mayor Carrington and Detective Furlong—and Bernie was going to prove it.

CHAPTER TWENTY-TWO

The first thing Erin felt was pain, a sharp stabbing in her chest that shot through her body, making every nerve scream. She convulsed violently, uncontrollably, and through the haze, realized that she was swinging freely. And then the pain suddenly stopped. The muscles in her shoulders and arms were still on fire, but the rest faded back down to bearable. She swung to a halt, and opened her eyes.

She was in the center of a warehouse, hanging from a crossbeam by her bound wrists. Her feet were about six inches above the ground. Most of her armor was gone. All that remained was her mask and her bodysuit, which had been unzipped down to her navel. Inches away from the skin of her chest was a handheld Taser. Holding it was Mr. Chaos.

"Oh good, you're awake. I wasn't sure how many times I was going to have to zap you before you came to." He moved over to a chair, and sat down. "That shock was your own fault. I tried to remove your mask, and got quite a jolt for my efforts. I simply had to return the favor."

She wanted to say something witty and sarcastic, but her mouth was dust-dry, and she could only manage a croaking sound.

"That sounds horrible. Would you like some water?" He picked up a plastic bottle from a folding table beside him. "You'll have to tell me how to take your mask off, though. Unless you want me to just pour it in those air-slits."

"Fuck... off..." she forced out.

"Oh, such language." He stood, and hit her in the bare stomach with the Taser.

She writhed in pain again, flailing around like a fish on a hook. Every muscle in her body shrieked. The only reason she didn't scream was that her dry throat wouldn't let her. The shock could only have lasted a few seconds, but it felt like an hour. As soon as it stopped, her body went limp again. She couldn't stop herself from sobbing.

"You are obviously in *way* over your head here." Chaos put the Taser on a table. Next to it was the rest of her gear. "I'm not going to lie to you. You're going to die. You have to. It's just the way it is. What you *can* control is how much pain you endure before I kill you. My original plan was to just kill you at the celebration, but then I started thinking about your gear. It's really nice stuff, better than anything I have. You're not a thinker, so I'd like to meet the person who made it for you. Tell me who it is and how to find them, and I'll kill you quickly. What do you say?"

It took her every ounce of strength to raise her head up, but she looked Chaos in the eyes, and shook her head.

"Fine." He slammed a fist into her stomach, smashing all the air out of her lungs. "I'm cool with doing this the hard way."

He turned back to the table and shifted some stuff before snapping back around holding her escrima sticks. She couldn't see it through his mask, but she knew he was smiling.

"I noticed that the weave in your bodysuit absorbs force. Which explains how you were able to shake off some of my hits." He swung one of the sticks through the air. "I was wondering just how much force it stopped. Let's find out, shall we?"

Chaos smashed the stick into her right side, hard. The suit barely stopped her ribs from breaking. He followed it with strikes to her left arm, her right thigh, and her chest. The suit soaked up some of the force, but far too much got through. He kept going, hit after hit slamming into her. Her mouth flooded with blood and bile, but the mask prevented her from spitting it out.

There was nothing she could do.

He just kept hitting her, over and over. The legs, the stomach, the ribs, the chest, the arms, each strike more painful than the last. Somewhere around fifty, she lost count.

When he did finally stop, he moved in close, his mask touching hers. "Are you ready to talk yet?"

She couldn't move her head. All she wanted was to curl up in a ball and pass out. But she dredged up every shred of defiance and hate she had. "No."

It was barely a whisper, but it made him laugh. He pulled a knife out of his boot and cut the rope that held her wrists. She dropped to the floor and fell forward, but Chaos grabbed her by the head and pulled her back up to a kneeling position.

"Let's see what our little work-out did." He moved behind her and pulled her suit down off her shoulders.

Cold air stung her from the waist up. All the skin she could see was covered in furious red welts. She could barely force air into her lungs, and the taste of blood and vomit was strong. The black of unconsciousness was creeping in around the edges, and she wasn't sure why she was bothering to resist it. She didn't think she had any fight left in her, but she'd be damned if she was going to give up Mr. Johnson, or take off her mask. Her final act of defiance.

A cell phone rang. "One moment," he said, and retrieved it from the table. He sighed, and answered. "This isn't a good time. What? No, I did exactly what I said I was going to. Look, hang on, I have terrible reception in here."

Chaos let go of her shoulder, and walked towards the exit. Erin fell forward again nervelessly, her mask smacking hard into the cement floor again. Her body was screaming in pain, blackness was pushing in, and all she wanted to do was to let go of it all. But she couldn't. She always kept going. Even after she'd left the service, she'd never given up. Now that she finally had a few things going for her, some lunatic was *not* going to take it all away.

She didn't have any strength to move, but she had all the rage that had been building up inside of her for years. This was her life, and she wasn't ready to just give it up become some whack-job in a mask wanted to make a name for himself. No way in hell was she going to let that happen. Not for him. No, she was going to get up. Fuck Mr. Chaos.

She forced her arms under her body, and slowly pushed herself back up to her knees. Every move sent new waves of nauseating pain through her. She grabbed the edge of the chair, and used it to help pull herself up off the ground. Her legs refused to stop shaking, so she hung on to the table. She moved as quickly as she could—she only had moments—but it was still a snail's pace. Once she could stand, she gathered up the stuff on the table. All her gear was there, including the Wishmaster, but he'd emptied the magazine.

She looked around the warehouse and saw a series of offices over on the left, and headed for them at top speed. It was little more than a shamble, every step an agonizing eternity. He had to be there. He was surely about to speak up, something mocking. But somehow she got across the warehouse and into what turned out to be a staff room, with tables, a refrigerator, a sink, a microwave, and a row of lockers. A metal fire door led onwards, away from the warehouse floor. Inside a locker, she found a pair of overalls, a backpack and some sneakers. The backpack held an L.A. Dodgers hat, a purple t-shirt and an energy drink.

She slipped out of her suit and took off her mask. They went into the backpack with the Taser and the rest of her gear. Then she pulled on the t-shirt, overalls and sneakers. It was all a couple sizes too big, but who cared. She slammed back the energy drink as she dressed, and then put on the hat.

His voice echoed from the other room. "Son of a bitch!"

She heard him running across the cement floor. She popped open the fire door, going dizzy with relief for an instant when she saw the street beyond it. Turning away, she lurched over to the lockers, slipped inside one, and closed it just as the staff room door was flung open. Through the locker's slits, she saw Chaos enter the room. He glanced around for a moment, then raced out the door.

Erin stayed exactly where she was.

After a few minutes, she slipped out of the locker. He wasn't visible outside. She grabbed the backpack, and went back into the warehouse. At the back, a row of crate-filled pallet racks stacked up to the ceiling. She put on the backpack, and began to painfully climb the side of the row. Her arms somehow stayed in their sockets, and once at the top, she crawled across the crates until she found one with some room behind it. She squeezed down between the crate and wall, out of sight, and set the backpack down on the racking. Then she lowered herself to lie there next to it, using it as a pillow, and wrapped her arms around herself. Pain thudded through her, in time with her heartbeat.

She'd been there a few minutes when she heard his boots stomping across the floor. "It's me. She's gone. Oh I don't know, maybe it's because you just *had* to call to whine at me like a little bitch. Oh, shut up. You didn't die. Get over it. Round up some loyal guys right this instant and have them start driving around the area of 1st and Murphy. If they see any blond who looks beat up, they grab her. Yes, very beat up. She's too hurt to have gotten far. Yes, of course I have. Now I need to move my stuff and get set up somewhere else. I'll call you when… What? Hell, no! I'm not going anywhere until I've killed her. No. Look, I don't give a damn what you think. Ugh, fine. I'll try to do it quietly. I said I'd *try*. Keep the hell out of my way, or else." He stopped talking. The phone hit the table.

Erin lay as still as she possibly could. She couldn't afford any kind of sound. Fighting was out of the question—hell, she couldn't even walk. All she could do was hope he went away.

She listened as Chaos moved about the warehouse. There was a bit of rattling and scraping. After a few minutes, she heard him stomp to the far side, where he'd gone out to talk earlier. The door slammed shut, and an engine started up and then faded away. She let out a sigh of relief, and finally allowed herself to fade away.

When she awoke, she had no idea of the time. Every inch of her body felt like hammered crap, and all her muscles had gone stiff. Every move was a new level of excruciating pain. She pushed through it as silently as she could. After pulling the backpack on, she crawled across the crates and slowly climbed down. At the bottom, she listened closely. Dead quiet. She made her way across to the staff room, noticing that the table and chair had gone. A second pass through the lockers turned up a little over five dollars in singles and change. There was a slice of pizza in the fridge, and she wolfed it down almost without chewing. It tasted wonderful.

She opened the side exit, surprised that it was dark. Still? Again? Just how long had she been there? It didn't really matter. She started walking back towards downtown as quickly as her battered body could move.

A block later, she spotted a taxi cab at a light. She slid into the back seat, surprising the driver.

"Oh, hey. Where to?"

She gave him the address of the trailer park, but not the specific unit.

He glanced back at her, sized her up, and frowned. "It'll be about ten dollars."

She held up the cash she'd scavenged. Her arms were spectacularly bruised. "I have five dollars and eight-two cents. I really need to get home. Please."

He stared at her for a long moment. "Is home where you really need to go?"

She nodded. "Really."

He smiled finally. "It's a slow night, and you are a Dodgers fan."

She passed him the money with a thankful smile. He pulled away as the light turned, and a cop car passed them in the other direction. She ducked down a little in her seat.

"Were you there last night?" the cabby asked.

"You mean the celebration? No, I wasn't."

"I wasn't either, had to work. But man, I've been hearing about it all day." He glanced at her in the mirror as he drove. "Lots of people got hurt. Plenty of folks been blaming the Sting for showing up. Saying no one woulda gotten hurt if she'd just stayed home."

She blinked at that. "That doesn't seem fair. How would she know Chaos was going to show up?"

"Well, he wouldn't ever had come to Blythe if it wasn't for her. Not saying that's how I feel, just what I've been hearing."

There was nothing much she could say to that. They rode in silence for a while, until he pulled up outside the park. "Here's your stop. Be safe, ok?"

She thanked him and got out. As she hobbled towards her trailer, she turned it over in her mind. She wasn't sure how she felt about being blamed for what Chaos had done. Maybe they were right. She was too tired to really think about it. For now, all she wanted was to get home and sleep for a week. Everything else would have to wait until after that. Including finding Mr. Chaos and returning some of the pain he'd given her.

CHAPTER TWENTY-THREE

Bernie sat at his desk, working through the Mayor's copied data and fretting about the Sting. He hadn't heard anything since she'd been taken by Chaos. No comments from the City. Back at the diner, all the other patrons had been talking about the massacre. A lot of them seemed to think it was her fault that Chaos had attacked. He'd retreat to his office before he started shouting at them.

It took him a while to really make headway on what he was seeing in the data. The property purchases made simple sense, but there was so much more to unravel. Such as a series of shelf companies that Carrington had set up, a series of entities created and then put on a shelf until they were needed. Some of them had been used to buy land across the city. Others were waiting, ready to go. It was an extremely elaborate setup and from everything he could tell, all perfectly legal.

But the companies had been created before the memo listing the candidate cities had been written. There was no reason to create a dozen or more interlinked companies without knowing about Project: Camelot. It was the only justification for buying up land in Blythe. Which meant that Carrington must have had someone on the inside who'd given him the information. Someone close to Quentin West. Where had that knowledge come from? And who'd known enough and had enough access to send West's letter on to the Blythe Bulletin?

There were other files, ones that Bernie found more upsetting, that showed the crime rate in the city broken down by neighborhood. Before Camelot, the numbers had been fairly static across the board, some places better, some worse, but all basically level. But they began to change around the same time as the Mayor's companies became active. Crime rates rose at least ten percent everywhere, but up to twenty-five percent in certain nicer neighborhoods, and on rotation too.

A second document showed police patrol routes over the months. The correlation was clear. They picked an area and moved the patrols out.

The crime rate went up, and not long after, house prices went down. Then the shell companies bought up anything that hit the market. Once house sales died off, they moved the patrols back in, stripping the next target area.

He'd started hearing rumors about the meth lab in the trailer park around the time all of this started. One of the shooters the Sting had brought in had been a cop, and it made dark sense that part of Carrington's plan would involve directly boosting the crime rate. But there was nothing in the files to prove that connection.

And that was the real problem.

Anyone looking at the data would see that the mayor was forcing down the property values in the city in order to make a fortune if West brought his project there. But the files were completely inadmissible. A USB drive left by a masked vigilante on a car's window was well outside the for the standards of evidence for any court of law.

Bernie could certainly show West what was going on. But then the billionaire would just pick a different city for the project, and although that would screw over Carrington, it would also screw the people of Blythe. The same would happen if he ran the data as a story in the Bulletin, except he'd *also* get sued for libel and investigated for possession of the files. He didn't even have the Sting to corroborate where the data had came from. The whole thing was insanely frustrating.

Maybe he couldn't deal with the corruption. However, he could at least address the events of the Key ceremony, and he would do it in the way he knew best… with his words. He started a new post and began to type.

The Fleeting Light of Hope

The city of Blythe is 140 years old. It was founded in 1877 by a former Union Soldier named William Calloway, who used the Swamp Land Act of 1860 to secure the area. The irony of that Act being used to establish a city in the desert shouldn't be lost on anyone. Calloway convinced a Welshman named Blythe to invest in this new empire by the Colorado River.

The region had a lot of problems right from the start, including periodic floods and attacks by natives. One such attack killed Calloway in 1880. Blythe himself only visited the area twice, and left his heirs to fight over his estate.

Things picked up a little when the railroad came to town. During World War II, the Army set up an Air Force base here. That helped. Then in the early 1970s, Interstate 10 was run through the center of town, and things took a turn for the worse. People stopped riding the trains. Cars began to speed past, and kept on going to Los Angeles or Phoenix. At best, we became a place to fuel up and grab a snack before getting back on the road. Even that has waned, now that gas prices are twenty cents cheaper on the other side of the border. The closest thing we've had to new business in the area is a trickle of marijuana farmers.

There isn't a lot to get excited about if you live here. There isn't a lot to give us hope. The crime rate is climbing and the police don't seem to be able to make a difference. The housing market is plummeting. Unemployment levels are horrendous. And the best place to get tacos shut down two months ago. It was starting to feel like we were stuck in quicksand, with no hope of getting out.

And then there was a literal bang. A masked woman, leaping away from an exploding meth lab. A woman brave enough to step in and make a difference when law enforcement would do nothing. A woman who broke up a bank robbery, stopped a drive-by shooting, and defused a hostage situation that had already cost two lives. A woman that we came to call the Sting. She stood for the people of this city in a way that no one has for a very long time. She put her life on the line to make a difference — something that even Mayor Carrington recognized and tried to honor.

We all know how that went horribly wrong. At this moment, all we know is that she was abducted by an insane mass-murderer. There have been no sightings of the Sting or of the homicidal killer who shot up the event. If the police know anything, they're not sharing it. She may well be dead.

Friday night was a tragedy. Innocent people lost their lives, and many more were injured. Good friends of mine died. The murderer needs to be found and made to pay for his actions. But I've been hearing a lot of negativity towards the Sting for showing up. People are saying that it was as much her fault that this happened. The same people who were cheering her actions just days before are now calling her a menace, a danger to this city, even claiming she deserves whatever has happened to her.

I actually heard one person suggest that the Sting is in it together with that murdering scum, in a conspiracy to rip off the city somehow. I'm not even going to pretend I understand the logic behind that one.

A hero is typically defined as someone who is admired for their courage, outstanding achievements and noble qualities. But that definition is too fleeting for modern times, in my opinion. Public emotion changes with the wind, driven by the latest news cycle. Someone admired today is just as easily ostracized tomorrow. To me, a hero is someone who is willing to stand up and do the right thing regardless of how it affects them personally.

The Sting risked her life multiple times. She risked being arrested to take down a cop killer. When she was asked to come and receive our thanks, she was attacked by someone the police should have had in custody. Even then, she protected the mayor, and did everything she could to keep the lunatic's focus on her so as many bystanders as possible could get away. She has done everything a hero could possibly do, and she may have paid the ultimate price for it. Yet there are people in this city talking badly about her for her heroism.

Maybe it's us. Maybe we don't know what to do when someone is standing up for us. Maybe we don't know how to keep the fleeting light of hope alive. Or maybe we've just become so cynical that we can't even believe in hope when it does come into our lives. When you're kicked over and over again, you assume that every movement is another kick coming in. If that's what we've become, then it breaks my heart. I know there are good people in this city. People who deserve to have good things happen. For the first time in a long time, we had something good — and now it may have been taken away, and the only way we know how to react is to make like it was a bad thing all along.

The Sting is a hero, and I pray that she is alright. I pray for her sake, and for the sake of this city.

He finished the article and read it over again. He wasn't sure about posting it. He believed every word, and felt that the city needed to read it. But was the Bulletin the right venue? Since he'd started it, he'd made it a rule to tell the facts, and leave opinions to the readers. The media's job was to inform, not to manipulate or entertain, and way too much of the mainstream media came with an agenda. Turn on one cable news network, and the world was great and the government was doing everything right. You moved up one channel, and the entire economic structure of the nation was on the verge of collapse and the nation needed a coup. Change the channel again, and the ice caps were melting and we'd all be dead in twenty years; flip back, and the EPA was too restrictive and the word 'clean' belonged next to the word 'coal'. That wasn't how the media was supposed to work.

A time when the president was saying, "Don't believe what you hear and read," and a former New York City Mayor was telling people that "the truth isn't the truth," and trying to sell the idea of "alterative facts," seemed a dangerous moment to set aside standards and let personal bias in. Bernie believed in the Sting and what she was trying to do. He also believed that if the worst had happened and she was gone, the people of Blythe would be the ones to really lose. She had been starting to make a difference, but things would get worse if she was gone. There would be no one left to stand up to Carrington and his corrupt friends.

He reread the article. It was a good piece, and it got his feelings across well. But it was an opinion. He didn't publish opinions. He took a deep breath and archived it. Then he started typing a fresh piece, relaying what he'd seen at the ceremony — his account of the crowd, the way the police had acted, what had happened once the Sting had arrived, and the things she'd done. He laid out the facts in vivid detail, with the number of casualties and the names that had been made public. Public opinion and who to blame would have to be for readers to decide.

Once it was done and proofed, he posted it, and then cleaned up the office. The computer and the drive went into his hiding place. Finally, he locked up and headed out to his car. It wasn't that late, but he didn't feel like being exposed to any more people, so he hit a drive-thru for a burger and fries before heading home. After eating, he texted a couple of his sources on the force trying to find out something new, and then settled down on his couch and fell asleep listening to the ugly commentary of the police scanner.

CHAPTER TWENTY-FOUR

Erin adjusted her position in bed and groaned loudly. "Son of a bitch!" Every breath made her wince, but that was nothing compared to the agony of trying to move. Even lying perfectly still and taking super-shallow breaths made her body ache.

More sleep clearly wasn't going to happen. She gingerly eased herself out of the bed, and hobbled to the couch. She ran her fingers over her ribcage nervously, trying to see if there were any breaks. It was crazy not to go to the hospital, but the police were almost certainly checking patients to see if any fit the Sting's description. She suddenly regretted that her short blond hair stuck out the top of her mask.

Once she was up to it, she limped over to the refrigerator for a bottle of water and a bag full of ice. She wrapped a dishcloth around the bag, and when she got back to the couch, she placed it against her side. After a painful swig of the water – even swallowing hurt – she booted her laptop up. Had the cabby had been right about people blaming her? Blythe rarely made the news, but a shooting like that should've at least hit the local stations if not the cable news networks.

She started with the Bulletin. Bernie had covered the event with professional detachment. That was an amazing feat, since he had been right in the middle of it all. But the article was straight forward and factual.

Then she made a mistake, and looked at the comments. Even as she scrolled down, she knew it was a mistake, that comment sections were havens for trolls, but she couldn't help herself. She had to see what people were thinking.

A good number of the responses were a simple waste of time. No one cared who'd been first to post, and she wasn't looking for dietary supplements. Quite a few posts were about her ass, and ranged from vulgar compliments to the term "white girl booty," which was apparently an insult. One poster suggested that she was a guy and wore armor that looked female to gain a tactical advantage. Another claimed that she didn't actually exist, but at the same time that she was a tool of the 'deep state.'

The responses that got to her were the ones talking about innocent bystanders who had been hurt, and how her showing up had put them all in harm's way. One woman posted about her cousin who'd gone to the celebration to support the Sting and was now in intensive care with life-threatening bullet wounds. There was a crowd-funding account already set up to help with the medical bills. Erin wanted to donate, but she just didn't have any money to give. There was a picture of the cousin, a girl in her early twenties with a big smile on her face. It was heartbreaking.

She continued to read. Some people did defend her, or put all the blame on Chaos. Others felt it had been her responsibility to protect them, regardless of what the killer had done. Every self-doubt she'd had over the last few weeks was in there. What right did she have to take the law into her own hands? Wasn't she just asking for trouble? Wasn't she putting people at risk and inviting criminals to challenge her? The number of people condemning her far surpassed those defending her.

Maybe the best thing she could do — for the town *and* herself — was to hang up the suit. Chaos would eventually give up if she wasn't there anymore. She'd made things worse for the city, and suiting up again would just compound it. Besides, she was broken and battered. She'd lost, badly. It was time to admit she didn't know what she was doing, and stop before any more people got killed.

She *really* wanted a drink. There were some beers in the refrigerator that she still hadn't touched. That made her stop for a moment. She hadn't had anything to drink in a while, hadn't even felt the urge for a beer. Not long ago, her only reason for getting up had been a six-pack. Maybe Hertzberg had been right about helping people being a positive thing for her. Of course, like everything in her life, she'd found a great way to screw it up.

That beer was calling her name, loudly.

It took her two attempts to get up off the couch. The first time, a bolt of blazing pain shot through her side and knocked her right back down. Her second attempt was slower, but more successful. Before she got to the kitchen though, there was a knock on the door. Other than Mr. Johnson, no one should have known that she was there. She moved as quietly as she could to the window, and peered out through the blinds. Blinking in surprise, she checked her sports bra was decent, then walked over to the door and flung it open, trying to hide the vicious stab in her ribs as she did so.

"You here to throw me out of town again?" she demanded, not bothering to hide the anger in her voice.

Robert stood at the bottom of the step, avoiding eye contact. "I'm sorry. I was wrong."

She stared at him. Where was the self-righteous 'I told you so,' or the angry 'what the hell were you doing?' The last thing she'd expected was an apology. She'd been furious every time she'd thought of him for days, and now, after everything had proved him right all along, he was apologizing. It didn't make sense.

"Can I come in?"

She took a step back, more out of habit than anything. He made his way up the stairs and into the trailer, a backpack on one shoulder. In the living room, he put the pack on the floor and took a seat in the plastic-covered armchair.

Erin levered herself painfully back down to the couch. "What do you want?" It came out harsher than she expected.

"I wanted to see if you were okay." He shifted in his chair nervously. "I talked with Mr. Johnson last night. He saw you come home, and told me where you were staying. I'd already planned to come talk to you before everything happened..."

"Why? Didn't you say everything you needed to on the drive to Indio?"

"You saved my life. I'm only here because of you." He made eye contact finally. "When I drove you out of town, I *thought* I was returning the favor. I was convinced you were on a path that would get you killed. What I hadn't realized was for the first time since we left the desert, you were alive again. That becoming the Sting made you whole. When I saw the footage of you taking on that psychopath, it was like watching you race in to battle, all over again. The thing that had been killing you was you living on my couch, trying to exist in a mundane world. You were doing what was right for you. I just couldn't handle my best friend becoming a vigilante."

She stared at him for a moment, and then laughed. "That sounds like a bad after-school special."

"Oh God, it does." He laughed as well.

With the laughter, a lot of the tension drained from the room. He noticed the bruises along her ribs and chest, nodded to himself, and reached for his backpack. Opening it up, he pulled out a fast food bag, put it on the table, then dug back into the pack for a smaller black bag.

"You brought food?" she asked.

"Thought you might be hungry. Burger and fries."

"Hot damn." She reached over and took the bag carefully, fished out the food, and started eating.

"I've also got my first aid kit, and a few things that might take the edge off the pain." He tapped the black bag. "Assuming those bruises are real, and not just make-up to help with the macho image."

"They're definitely real." She slowly lifted her arm so he could see the full extent of the damage. "I now know what a punching bag feels like."

He shook his head in disbelief. "I hope you gave as good as you got."

She turned back to the food. "Sadly, no. I walked into a trap and I'm lucky to be alive. And because of that, people got killed, people whose only mistake was thinking I was worth celebrating."

He got moved to the couch next to her. "An asshole who was supposed to be in police custody uses an event put on by the mayor to try and kill you, and that's your fault how?"

"If I hadn't shown up then... OWWW!"

Robert was pressing on her side, looking for breaks.

She smacked weakly at his hand, but he didn't stop.

"Do you mind, I'm working here."

"Do I mind? You're not the one in pain."

"Are you kidding? Just looking at these bruises is painful." He pressed again, eliciting another groan of pain.

"I will beat you." She shook her head. "As soon as I'm strong enough to make a fist."

"I'm not feeling anything broken, other than your logic." He pulled out a large cloth bandage. "But I'm going to wrap your ribs, just to be on the safe side."

"What do you mean my logic?" she said, between bites of the burger.

"You're blaming yourself for the attack, but you're missing a really important part of what I said."

She thought about it for a moment, then stopped chewing. "He was supposed to be in police custody."

"Ding ding. We have a winner." Robert finished wrapping the bandage, and pulled it uncomfortably tight. "From what I understand, every cop in the city was at the celebration. Why?"

"... Because they already knew he'd escaped." She stared at him. "They let it go on, hoping to recapture him. They were using those people as bait."

"Those people and *you*," he reminded her. "If you'd known Chaos was on the loose, would you have gone to the ceremony?"

"Hell no," she shot back.

"Exactly — because you care more about the people in this city than the police or the mayor do." He used metal clips to fasten the bandage. "You are amazing at blaming yourself for things. It may be your superpower. But you're not to blame for what happened. Everything you've done has been to help people. Except using my paintball gear. That still kind of sucks. But everything else you did for the right reasons. Stop beating yourself up."

"Interesting choice of words, but I get what you mean." She started to pull herself up. "I need to get out there and find Chaos before he hurts anyone else."

Robert gently stopped her from rising. "Nope. You need to rest. Go out like this, and he'll just kick your ass again. I'm going to give you some painkillers that should make you sleep through the night. After that you can go hunting."

"You're not the boss of me." She smiled.

"No, I'm your friend, and if you're going to go out and risk your life, I'm going to try to give you the best chance of coming back alive." He pulled a bottle from the black bag, took out two pills, paused, and then grabbed a third before handing them over.

She popped them in her mouth and washed them down with water. "This is probably for the best. I'm fairly sure with the condition I'm in, I couldn't pull my suit on."

"I was going to ask you about your suit." He put the bottle away. "Do you know there are whole discussion groups online dedicated to how your ass looks in that suit?"

"I saw some of that! What the hell is 'white girl booty'?"

"A flat butt." He ran his hand over the top of the table. "Flat as a piece of paper."

"My butt is not flat!"

"Well..."

She grabbed a handful of fries and threw them in his face. "Don't you dare!"

"Maybe it's just how tight the suit is. Have you thought about putting some padding in there?" He cupped his hands. "Go a bit more Kardashian?"

She shook her head. "I think I liked it better when we weren't talking to each other."

CHAPTER TWENTY-FIVE

After a second night — and a solid ten hours of sleep — Erin was feeling quite a bit better. She was still sore as hell and moving slowly, but it wasn't nearly as bad as it had been. She packed her gear into a bag, and carried it over to Mr. Johnson's trailer, being careful not to annoy her ribs. The old man was out front watering his petunias, and gave her a quick wave as she approached. The sun was just coming up in the east, which gave her a few hours before having to be at work.

"Glad to see you up and about." Johnson turned off the faucet.

"Thanks." She tapped her bag. "I think it's all in one piece but I'd appreciate you giving it the once-over, just to be sure."

He nodded. "Come on in. The coffee should be ready, and I've got a few sweet-rolls from the store."

She followed him into the trailer. He pointed to the table, then made his way to the kitchen where he poured two cups of coffee. She took a seat, and put the bag on the floor next to her. He returned with the coffee, a small carton of creamer, and a plastic-wrapped package of sweet-rolls with a variety of fillings. He put everything down, then picked up her bag and took a seat on the opposite side.

She poured a generous amount of cream into her coffee and added a couple packs of sugar that were already on the table. Then she opened the pastries, and selected one with a cherry filling. She offered them towards the old man, but he was already examining the mask.

"How'd the lock work?" he asked.

"Fine." She smiled. "He wasn't very happy about the shock it gave him."

"Good."

"The suit held up great. The problem came when he had me bound, and took it off me."

"He did what?" Anger flashed across his face. "He didn't..."

"No." She shook her head. "He noticed that the suit was absorbing the majority of his blows. He was really impressed and wanted to know

139

who made it. When I refused to tell him, he pulled the top down enough to try and torture it out of me with a Taser. I never told him."

He looked her in the eye. "Thank you."

She sipped her coffee while he pulled out the main part of the suit and examined the collar where the zipper fastened. "I could create a collar that would prevent anyone from opening the suit, put the same fingerprint lock on it."

"Let's put that on the to-do list for the future." She smiled. "I need to make sure the suit is good to go as soon as possible."

"You plan on going after Chaos?"

"No." She took a bite of her sweet-roll. "I plan on him coming after me."

He pulled the rest of the pieces from the bag. "You'd better start from the top."

"I guess I haven't caught you up. I'll give you the short version." She took a quick swig of coffee. "I've been working with Bernie Green over at the Blythe Bulletin on a tip he got about a plan to revitalize one area of California. Project: Camelot. Blythe is one of the contenders. The information got leaked to the Mayor and a few others, who have been trying to drive folks out of the area and buy up the cheap land. When I popped up, it threw a wrench into their machinations. My working theory is that they brought in Mr. Chaos to deal with me. Otherwise it would be just a huge coincidence."

"And there are no coincidences, right?"

"Right." She nodded. "At one point I broke into Carrington's office and swiped some information off his computer. It shows the land he's bought up, and how they've been shifting police coverage away from areas they want to buy. Bernie figured it all out. Because the information was stolen, and came to him from the Sting, it's tainted. We can't take it to the feds, and if we made it public, the guys wanting to refurbish the city would just stay away, screwing the mayor and friends, but also everyone else in the city."

"This all looks to be in good shape." He pushed the suit back into the bag, then turned to face her. "You know what's going on, but can't do anything about it. That's got to be frustrating as hell."

"That's putting it mildly. But although I can't go to the authorities, I do have an idea. I was hoping we could make an adjustment or two to the mask, and then I'll confront them again." She explained what she was looking for him to do.

He reached his hand over and put it on hers. "They've already tortured you and tried to kill you. Is it really a good idea to bait them again?"

"That was the whole purpose of this, wasn't it? For me to go out there and try to help people?"

"Yes — but in the safest way possible. That's why I built the suit, to give you the best chance to survive. But the suit can only do so much. You making yourself an even bigger target?" He pulled his hand back. "I don't like the idea at all."

"I know it's not a great plan." She laughed softly. "It's not even a good one. But it's the only one we have. Our first priority is getting Chaos off the streets, but if he's working with the cops, then just having him arrested again won't solve anything. We have to take them all down at once, and in a way that doesn't spill the beans on Project: Camelot."

The old man sat quietly for a minute, staring in her direction and pursing his lips over and over. Eventually, he sighed. "Fine. I can have the modifications done in about twenty minutes. What else do you need?"

"Thank you." She reached for a second pastry. "I could use your help recording two videos. And do you think there's any way we can get the motorcycle back?"

"Its already in the storage unit." It was his turn to smile. "I was at the ceremony. Figured it would be fun to see you get the key to the city. I was way in the back when everything happened. I saw you get taken. While everyone was running around, I made way over to the bike, hopped on and drove it back. I'd just have gotten my ass kicked or killed if I'd tried to help you, but I figured I could at least keep the cops from getting the bike."

"Excellent." She pulled an apple-filled pastry from the bag. "That's going to make this a lot easier."

Rock sat in his office, his emotions churning. The video he'd been linked should've enraged him. It put all of his plans at risk. But at the same time, it also offered a very real opportunity to solve almost all of his problems. He'd have to play it just right — and rely on their lunatic to do something — but he could see how it should all work out in the end.

The intercom buzzed. "They're here," Audrey said.

"Send them in."

Spanky and Furlong entered together. The cop looked dreadful, shell-shocked and wired, like he'd been up all night chugging coffee and slamming his head into desks. The gangster just looked half-asleep. They took their usual seats.

He said nothing until they were settled, then turned to the cop. "Any word on Chaos?"

"Nothing." Furlong sneered. "I've told my men to shoot first. We'll make everything right once he's in the ground."

"Change that order. We need him alive."

"What!" The detective leapt to his feet in protest. "He killed my men! He made me look like an idiot! I want him in a body bag!"

Carrington forced himself to speak soothingly. "Of course. You'll kill him. Just not yet. We need him for one more thing. After that, you can turn him into Swiss cheese for all I care."

Furlong sat back down huffily. "They're *my* men. He doesn't get away with killing them."

Sure, Wade. You're delighted to kill them any time you like, no-one else can, right? Rock wasn't sure of the logic there, but it was certainly consistent. He turned to the gangster. "You think you can get a message to that lunatic?"

"Yeah, no problem." He popped a toothpick into his mouth. "But whether he'll listen to it or not is anyone's guess."

"He'll listen." The mayor smirked at the thought. "He wants another shot at that bitch, and we're going to provide it."

Furlong snapped forward. "How? No-one's seen her."

"I have." He held up his phone. "Turns out Miss Goody-Two-Shoes isn't all that virtuous after all. She sent me a message this morning. She knows all about Project: Camelot, us buying land, even Mr. Chaos being brought in to deal with her."

The two men on the other side of the desk said, in unison, "Holy shit!"

"Relax." He gestured for them to stay calm. "This is a good thing. She wants a cut. She'll come on-side in exchange for twenty percent of what we make. She also wants to take down our masked killer."

"Wait." Spanky held up his hand. "Why is she only asking for twenty percent? If she thinks she has us over a barrel, then why not ask for half?"

"It was part of her proof that she knew what was going on. She knew that there were four major figures involved. She asked for five percent off each of us, so she'd be an equal partner. Which means she knows about our mysterious friend. Besides, by being reasonable, she avoids forcing us to kill her. Twenty percent is a big hit, but there's enough to go around."

Furlong frowned. "She'd still be a pain in our ass. As long as she's on the street, the city has hope, and people don't move."

"She bought that up too." He gestured at his computer. "She must have been the vandal in my office the other night. She knew that we have almost all of the target property. But she also admitted that the Feds wouldn't accept the evidence because of how she got it. She's willing to coordinate with us to avoid propping up target areas. Maybe set up a few easy heroic moments for her, and she'll let the rest go. Work with your men to make them look better, too."

The detective sat back in his chair pensively. "That... actually sounds doable. And maybe the selection committee will like the idea of choosing a city with its own hero."

Spanky nodded. "True. And if our mysterious friend doesn't come through and the committee goes elsewhere, could be a tame hero would pull up property prices enough to get at least some profit."

The mayor nodded. "It's got potential. So I've set up a time and place for the showdown." He pushed a piece of paper over towards Spanky. "Let Chaos know this is his last chance to finish her."

The gangster looked at the paper then back to the mayor. "You want him to kill her? I thought we were making a deal with her?"

"We are." He smiled widely. "If she beats Chaos, we have a deal worked out. If Chaos beats her, then the cops move in and kill Chaos and we don't have to share our money. It's a win-win no matter how you look at it."

The detective stood. "What if she kills Chaos and then the cops kill her?"

"I don't see a problem with that either."

Erin arrived at the Blythe Bulletin right on time. Between the pain pills Robert had given her and keeping her movements slow and simple, she felt she could keep Bernie from figuring out just how badly she was injured. He was too bright for some lame story like her having fallen over in the shower. The best approach was to make it seem like nothing was wrong. She needn't have worried about it though. He was so distracted when she walked in that he didn't even notice she was there.

He was sitting at his desk, staring at the phone in his hand. His eyes were wide, and he had a small grin on his face. Since they still hadn't finished building her desk, she took a seat in the chair opposite him and waited.

She sat there quietly for a solid minute before finally speaking. "Good morning."

"Huh! What?" He jumped slightly and dropped the phone onto the desk.

"I said good morning."

"Oh my god." He looked around in shock. "When did you get here?"

"About ten minutes ago," she exaggerated. "You seemed focused on whatever you were doing on the phone. I hope it wasn't those pictures of the mayor's secretary."

His face turned crimson. "No! I got a message from the Sting."

She forward up in her seat. "She's alive? No one has seen her."

"Yeah. She said she's fine, and has a plan for catching the killer, the mayor and all of his cohorts."

"Did she really say cohorts?" She knew damn well she hadn't.

"Well... no. That was my word. But she has a plan, and needs me to do something for her." He paused. "I just don't know if I should."

Erin blinked at that. "Why wouldn't you?"

He glanced out the window in the direction of the vacant lot. "You weren't there on Friday. She walked into a trap. It was horrible. She knew that the mayor was crooked, but she stood in front of him to save his life. She let that lunatic take her in order to save innocent people around her. We have no idea what he did to her. And now she's ready to jump right back into danger? I don't know if I can be part of letting that happen."

"From what I've seen of her, she's a grown woman." She reached over and took his phone, holding it up. "Its her choice whether or not to put herself in danger. Every time she puts on the mask, it's her decision. But what she is doing is dangerous, and it sounds like she's come to trust you. That can't be easy with what she's doing. She trusts you to do something to help the city. You don't have to do it, of course. But your decision won't change whether she decides to risk her life again. That'll happen anyway. You can be someone she can count on or not, but you are not responsible for what she is doing."

She watched as Bernie gazed out the window for another minute, his face conflicted. Then he turned to his computer and started writing an email. She couldn't see all of it, but she saw enough to know that he was going to play his part. All the pieces were falling into place.

He finished and hit send, then turned to her. "Okay. You're right. I've helped our local hero-slash-vigilante. How about we get that desk of yours built finally."

She winced inwardly at the thought of DIY with her ribs. "You're the boss."

CHAPTER TWENTY-SIX

The week passed quickly. By Friday, the night of the meet, Erin was starting to feel like herself again. She'd set the time for the meet to be Friday at midnight, giving her body time to heal before suiting up again. She'd scouted the location that the mayor had chosen. The King Ranch Corporation HQ was one of the largest buildings in the city. KRC was a farming company that grew melons and vegetables for produce markets. It was one of the few businesses that had continued to thrive through the rough economic times.

She'd made a trip there on Wednesday under the pretense of doing a column for the Bulletin. A vice-president of something or other took her on a tour of the facility and some of the farm area. She was sent home with a box full of cantaloupes, honey dews, watermelon, and brochures. She chopped up a huge melon salad to share with Bernie the next day, but made damn sure not to tell him where it came from.

Balancing a duel identity was very different to how it looked in the comic books.

Mr. Johnson had been making adjustments to the suit during the week. When she went to over the storage unit on Friday evening, she found him there, still hard at work at the bench.

"The modifications you asked for are ready." He didn't look up. "And there is a locking collar that works the same way as the mask. No electrical charge though."

"I appreciate that." She took a closer look at the suit. Three circular indentations now ran up the underarms of her gold forearm guards. "What's with the holes?"

"They're for these." He held up one of the small disks he was working on. "Mini-grenades. The three on the right arm are smoke, the three on the left are flash-bangs. They won't do any real damage, but they might provide a needed distraction. They're magnetically locked. Your gloves release them."

"Nice. How do I trigger them?"

"Concussion. Throw them against a wall or on the ground." He got up and walked over to the suit. He clicked one into place, and then touched the mask. "When you pull one of the flash-bangs, the lens automatically polarizes to counter the glare."

She ran her finger over the disc. "You are amazing."

"If I was amazing, I'd be able to talk you out of this plan." He clicked the others into place. "I'm guessing that's not an option?"

"No. It's not." She put her hand on his arm. "This needs to end before anyone else gets hurt."

"I know. Just be careful."

She took the suit and went behind the screen to change. As she zipped up the tight-fitting outfit, she realized that Johnson had also added some more armor over her ribs. It made her smile.

The old man had sat back down at the bench, and was putting his tools away. "Your plan B is also ready."

She nodded, opened the back door, and hopped on the bike. "See you later."

The ride down to Miller Park didn't take long. She entered off of Lovekin on the southeast corner, and silently rode her bike past the play area and baseball diamond to a crop of trees in the southwest, well hidden from the road. A quick fence-climb, and she was heading across an empty field towards the King Ranch building.

As she approached, she could see that the place was deserted. That made sense, it being midnight and the mayor having arranged to give the security guards the night off. She assumed she was being watched, so didn't bother trying to be stealthy. Instead, she headed straight for the open door.

Things had changed inside. Earlier in the week, the large warehouse had been pretty full, but with big open areas as well. Now everything was tighter. It wasn't horribly close, but all the produce that had been waiting outside had been brought in and stacked high, making the place feel like a maze.

"Over here!"

The sudden shout made her jump a little. She was more anxious than she'd realized, and she took a breath to calm herself before heading towards the sound of the voice. It took a couple of turns to find the mayor standing at the far end of a long row of pallets of produce. The goods were stacked solidly on either side and stretched about twenty feet up. It was like a long, skinny alley between two buildings made of melons. The space was maybe four feet across, and thirty feet long, and the hairs on the back of her neck immediately stood up at the sight of it.

Killzone. The little weasel was trying to screw her.

"I have to admit, I'm surprised you came," the mayor said.
"Why's that?"

He just smirked at her, and gestured with his right hand.

She heard movement, and caught a glimpse of a forklift as a stack of produce slotted in behind her, blocking her exit from the alley. The only way out was now on the other side of the mayor. "What the hell is this?"

"I believe you were looking for someone." He stepped to the side, and Mr. Chaos strolled into the alley.

The mayor backed out of the alley, and another forklift slid a stack of pallets in. Now they were boxed in. "You're a worthless piece of shit, Carrington!" she shouted. "And I never voted for you!"

She turned her attention to Chaos. He was in his usual outfit. He didn't have his staff with him this time, though. Instead, he carried two police batons held tonfa-style, with the long ends running back to his elbows. He lifted his arm so she could see one of them more clearly. "You like?" he asked. "I figured they'd be better for close-quarters fighting. I got them off of a couple dead cops."

"Of course you did." She shook her head. "Do we really have to go through this again? I beat you fair and square once, and then you beat me by cheating, and I still got away, even after you'd spent hours torturing me. Just admit you're outclassed, and go back to whatever city thinks that trench coats are still in fashion."

He looked down at his outfit. "What do you mean? This is a classic look. It'll never go out of style. And this is actually a duster. Notice the extra rain protection over the shoulders."

"And that's my point. You're wearing a raincoat in the desert." She kept her hands at her side, trying to keep the conversation going. "It's obvious you've never been here before, yet you're hooked up with Carrington and his dupes. Are you part of the land grab, or just a hired gun?"

"Stop talking!" The mayor yelled, from the other side of the produce wall.

She laughed. "Oh, yeah. Carrington doesn't want you to know that there's a *ton* of money to be made here if the city gets picked for the big revitalization project. Millions and millions of dollars for the people who bought up the land. Are you getting some of that?"

Chaos tilted his head to one side. "No," he said thoughtfully. "I'm just getting a flat rate."

"A flat rate? This is the third time you've had to fight me. Did they give you a realistic idea of what you were up against? Or even let you know why they wanted you to take me out?"

"Stop it! Stop listening!" The mayor sounded aggravated.

Chaos waved a hand towards the sound. "In a minute."

"You should hold out for a cut of the big money," she told him.

"Yeah, thanks." He turned to face the wall. "Hey!" he yelled. "I want a cut of the big money!"

She smiled under her mask. "You should get at least a third for all the work you're doing."

"Damn right! I want a third!" He punched one of the boxes of melons. "You hear me, Carrington?"

"Fine!" The mayor yelled back, openly angry now. "Just stop talking already, and...!"

Chaos pumped his fist in triumph. "Hot damn. Time to make the donuts."

"You believed that?" She scoffed. "He just folded, not even an argument. He's humoring you. Which tells me he has a bunch of cops out there waiting to gun down whoever wins this fight."

"Of course he does." He spun one of the batons in his hand. "But I can kill cops. Super easy. Barely an inconvenience. Let's get it on!"

Erin's plan went off the rails from there. She had barely enough time to get her sticks out and block as he leaped towards her for his first strike. The blow shuddered through her arm and down her side, making her ribs ache immediately. The moment the first baton connected, he began to spin around and swing the second one at her head. She was able to duck under it, but it left her off balance. He finished his spin to drive his right elbow into her face mask, sending her sprawling backwards into the wall of boxes.

"You are going to put up a fight, aren't you?" he asked sincerely. "I was hoping for one last good round before I killed you."

She pushed herself back onto her feet. "I'll try not to disappoint."

Chaos's batons were better for close fighting than his staff, but he still moved as if he had his staff, using extended fluid moves. She knew exactly how to press that advantage. She moved in, striking at his chest and face. Rapid blows, focused on a small area. It made his fluidity a hindrance. The best he could do was to keep the batons tucked against his arms, and use them to block. As she'd hoped, he pulled in close to guard the area she was repeatedly striking, so she switched up and launched a savage flurry at the sides of his head.

A few quick blows to the ears and temples sent him staggering backwards up the alley. He shifted his arms, opening up his center, and so she smashed a kick into his groin. The blow was so hard that it knocked him off his feet, and he crashed to the cement floor. She jumped up, tucked her knees in, and cannonballed squarely onto Chaos's chest. He gasped painfully for air, and dropped his batons.

She got to her feet. "This is your last chance, Carrington. Let me out of here and accept my deal, or I will rain *hell* down on you and your friends."

"You're a pathetic, deluded freak in bondage gear." Carrington yelled back. "The Blythe police will deal with you."

Chaos scrambled to his feet, gun in hand. She grabbed one of the flash-bang discs from her arm, and hurled it at his feet. The light in the warehouse seemed to waver, and he reeled. Her mask hadn't even let the noise through.

Mr. Johnson's upgrades had made the next phase much simpler. She grabbed two of the smoke discs and slammed them down on either side of her. The make-shift alley filled with fog. She aimed her grappling hook at some glass panes in the roof, ones she'd scoped out earlier in the week. The hook burst through, and secured itself to something outside. She clipped the gun back to her belt, hit the button, and zipped up into the night sky.

Once on the roof, she spoke into her mobile phone. "Did you get all of that?"

"Sure did." Bernie's voice sounded concerned. "It's a start..."

"Right." She ran across the roof towards the edge. "Well, I need to lead Chaos to a neutral place and end this."

Bernie replied immediately, sounding alarmed. "That wasn't part of the plan! Get out of there."

"The guy is going to just keep coming after me until I'm dead. He needs to go down permanently." She stopped at the edge and looked at the pavement below. "Don't worry. I've got this."

She turned the phone off before he could argue. From the roof, she leapt to the top of a semi-truck's trailer. As soon as her balance was solid, she ran the length of the truck, rolled down the windshield, and slipped off the hood to the ground. She sprinted across the open field to where she had parked her motorcycle, then scampered up and over the fence, hopped onto the bike, fired up the engine and waited.

Thirty seconds later, an unlit black SUV screeched out of the warehouse, Chaos clearly visible behind the wheel. As soon as she flashed her headlight at him, he floored the big Ford directly at her. She spun the bike around, and gunned it across the park. The SUV blasted through the chain-link fence, full beams flicking to life, and started tearing its way across the grass in pursuit.

She flew out of the park and onto the street, heading north, and grinned. It'd worked. Chaos was chasing her.

Now she just had to figure out where they were going.

CHAPTER TWENTY-SEVEN

Erin twisted the throttle full open, pushing the bike to its top speed. Chaos' black SUV was hanging steady in her rearview mirror. Her thoughts were racing ahead of her. Where could she lead the maniac to? It had to be somewhere that would be deserted but also afford her some cover. There weren't many places like that in Blythe. Then she realized she knew the perfect spot, and headed straight for it.

Slowing down just enough to send a quick text without crashing cost her most of her lead. She zipped past the front gate of the storage facility and then past the trailer park. She took a quick right and opened up the throttle again. Tires screeched behind her, but she didn't bother to look back. Another quick right, and she was headed back the other way. After a couple blocks she turned again, heading straight towards the now-open gate of the storage facility. She zipped inside, and the gate closed behind her. She headed to the back corner, leaped off her bike and ran into the maze units.

Ducking around a corner, she looked back to see Chaos slam to a stop at the driveway. He swiftly hopped out and jumped the fence. His coat swept around him like a cape as he dropped down into a fighting stance.

The lunatic pulled out his MP5, swinging it up to a ready position. Erin waited to see which direction he took, and then ducked back around the corner. She moved over to another aisle and lightly jogged to the next opening. She was amazed to discover her boots made no sound as she moved. Were they graphene, like her suit? Whatever technological magic it was, she was happy for it.

At the end of the row of units, she quickly poked her head around the corner. No one was there. She dashed across the empty space and then into the cover of the next row. She moved a little faster this time, getting to the end of the aisle near the front office and checking around the corner. Then she swung around by the front gate and looked up the first aisle. No sign of Chaos — but there was someone else standing next to the black SUV.

Bernie, filming everything on his cellphone.

She moved over to the fence. "What are you doing here?"

He kept his voice low as well. "Getting the story."

"You're going to get yourself killed." She glared at him, then remembered he couldn't see her face. "Get out of here."

"It's okay for you to risk your life but not for me to risk mine?" He continued filming. "Is this a reverse sexism thing?"

"What? No! I've got the suit and the weapons. You've got a camera and a plucky attitude. Plucky doesn't stop bullets."

Bernie's eyes went wide. "Get down!"

She turned. Chaos had backtracked, and was standing at the other end of the aisle. He opened fire. She quickly dove to the left, rolling over on her shoulder and back onto her feet just behind the storage units. She glanced back at the reporter, but he was out of sight. Hopefully he'd gotten away clean. Ripping the Wishmaster from its holster, she snap-fired three rounds towards the maniac. He shot back immediately. Bullets whizzed past her and into the front office window.

Scrambling to her feet, she ran past the next two aisles down to the final one and turned the corner. There she put her back against the inside row of units and waited, listening. His footsteps were just audible, running up the first aisle to where she had been. That gave her a few seconds. Her gun went back into the holster, and she moved across the aisle to get some distance, then ran straight for one of the units. The cement divider between the two metal roll-up doors gave her the height to leap up and grab the edge of the roof. She quickly pulled herself up and laid flat on her stomach. Crawling across to the other side of the building, she positioned herself where she could see Chaos as he approached. But he didn't.

His voice boomed out through the empty facility. "Is this how you want it to end? A ridiculous game of hide and seek?"

She stayed quiet, and pulled her gun back out. All she had to do was stay silent until he came into range.

"This doesn't work for me. I'm not a patient person." He began to whistle, badly.

Erin crawled a little closer to the corner of the building slowly, so as to make as little noise as possible. The roof was covered with pebbles and debris that shifted as she moved. Her new position allowed her to see the edge of his coat — he was standing by the front gate and pacing back and forth.

"All right, I'll make you a deal." He stopped pacing. "Let's finish this properly. No guns. Your sticks versus my staff. Right here in the storage unit. Your reporter buddy can film it all. You win, then I'm dead and you go back to your life as normal. I win, I promise I won't kill him after. But… If you don't agree, I'm going to hop back over this fence, find his nosy little ass, and kill him in the most painful way I can imagine. Trust me, I can imagine some pretty painful ways to kill someone. I doubt they'd even be able to put enough of him back together for a burial."

A second later, Bernie replied. "Don't do it. I can protect myself!" His voice rang with badly-faked bravado.

Chaos laughed loudly. "Oh my God! He's *adorable*. Please don't take my offer — he's going to be so much fun to torture."

Erin jumped back down, and silently jogged to the back of the facility, then around to the main aisle. She took a step out, holding her gun up in her left hand.

"Toss your gun over the fence," she shouted.

"How do I know you won't shoot me as soon as I do?" he asked.

"Because I'm the good guy."

Chaos nodded, and tossed his weapon over the gate, onto the hood of his SUV. She walked over to her bike and put the Wishmaster on the seat. Then she pulled out the escrima sticks, and ran through the Heaven Six sequence twice to loosen up. Chaos had his bo staff out, and was spinning it.

A voice from over the fence yelled, "I thought they only did that in kung-fu movies?"

Both fighters replied, in unison, "Shut up, Bernie!"

As she came to the end of her warm-up, Chaos stopped twirling his stick. Watching each other, they started walking forward slowly until they were just a few feet apart.

It was all very different from when she'd been in the Middle East. This wasn't another soldier willing to die for their country, another person doing a hard job for the other side. Chaos was genuinely crazy. He *enjoyed* killing people. He'd used innocent bystanders against her, multiple times. Though she hadn't thought about it at the time, she'd been holding back in her previous fights with him. She hadn't wanted to cross over into lethal force. It was a restriction that he didn't have. He would happily kill her, and everyone else around, just for the sake of it. If she'd had any lingering doubts, they were gone. There was only one way the fight could end. One of them was going to die.

She stood ready and looked straight into his eyes. "Let's do this."

He immediately swung his staff at her head. She used one stick on an upper swing to push the staff up, while she ducked low, spun around and slammed her other stick into his left knee. It buckled and he staggered but stepped away before she could follow up. As he moved back towards her, he thrust the staff forward at her chest. She crossed the sticks in front of herself and used them to push the staff up and to the side, sending the thrust harmlessly over her shoulder. It seemed to be what he wanted though, and he seized the opening to drive his knee up into her right side.

Though the suit absorbed a big part of the blow, her ribs were still in bad shape and she gasped for air.

"I meant to ask how your ribs were doing." He chuckled. "I bet they're still black and blue."

She took a step back, but brought her sticks up at the ready. Chaos was giving her a second to catch her breath. She wasn't sure why he wanted to prolong the fight. Over his shoulder she saw Bernie back in full view, holding his phone up to film. But now there were a couple more people standing with him.

Chaos glanced over his shoulder. "Ah, good. The audience is building. I prefer to work the big crowds."

Before she could respond, he swung his staff down hard toward her left knee. She smacked at it with her stick. It struck the ground and then bounced back up, and he drove it up into her ribcage again. Her eyes teared up as pain shot through her body. He was going to keep going for that spot until she left herself open for a kill shot. She could use that.

He feinted quickly, attempting to draw her forward and throw her off balance. She bit big time, turning her body to give him a clean shot at her wounded side and back. He swung his right fist towards the open spot. Rather than try to move back as he'd be expecting, she kept moving forward, and twisted hard to her right. His punch hit, glancing slightly to the side as her elbow slammed into his. Pain surged through her. She continued the spin, which carried her behind his back. As she went past, she tugged on the back of his mask, pulling it up in the front and covering his eyes. Using that moment of distraction, she swung her free stick into his mouth, and was rewarded with the sound of breaking teeth.

He staggered away, pulling at the mask until it came off his head. When he looked back up, his mouth was covered in blood, and he spit out a canine. "You bitch!"

For the first time, she saw his face. He had slicked-back black hair and thick eyebrows. High cheekbones and a lantern jaw would have given him a leading man look, if not for his nose, which looked to have been broken multiple times. Minus the blood, she'd almost have called him attractive. But she didn't know who he was. Then again, he probably wouldn't recognize her under her mask either.

"That was for the bullshit with the taser." She stood at the ready. "Shall we continue?"

"Just for that, I am going to kill the little geek once I'm done with you." He pointed at Bernie. "Don't bother to run. I'll find you."

Erin took the offensive, attacking with a series of rapid-fire strikes from multiple angles. Chaos was quick, and blocked a few with both his staff and his forearms, deflecting the rest enough to weaken their impact. But she was quick and fluid, and each block turned immediately into another strike. She needed to overwhelm him, force him to make a mistake. Her opening turned out to be a quick strike to this throat. He saw the blow coming, and twisted his head enough to take it on the side instead of directly in the windpipe. Still, it was enough to make him gasp for air.

She heard a cheer from the side and risked a glance towards the front gate. An even bigger crowd was gathered. "Are you people crazy? He'll kill you if he can! Go!"

Nobody moved.

She shook her head, and turned back to see the staff slamming into her face. It was a powerful blow, and it knocked her off her feet to slam shoulder-first into the pavement. One of her sticks went spinning off. The other got pinned under her body. The staff crashed into her exposed ribcage again. She cried out at the blaze of pain.

He raised the staff over his head, and before he could bring it down, she kicked up at his groin. He turned quickly enough so she hit his thigh instead. "I don't think so."

She flipped onto her back, freeing her remaining stick just in time to block his next strike. He'd over-extended himself, putting extra force into it. It left him slightly over-balanced. She grabbed the staff with her free arm, and twisted it. His grip faltered, and she ripped it out of his hand and tossed it down the aisle.

He took a step back and laughed. "You don't give up, do you?"

She got up on one knee. "Never."

"I'm tired of this." He reached inside his coat, and pulled out a Glock .45 ACP to point at her head. "Its time to kill you and the reporter. Then I'm going to go get pancakes."

"I thought you said no guns?"

"I'm the bad guy. I cheat." He took careful aim. "Any chance you want to tell me who made your suit?"

"Sure." She turned her shrug into a quick reach around her back. "The same guy who made this cool-ass grappling gun."

She whipped it round and fired. The hook blasted out of the gun and plunged into Chaos' chest two feet away, bursting out through his back in a spray of blood. His eyes widened with surprise and confusion. His gun fell from his hand, and he reached for his chest.

"What...? Y-Y-You...?!?" he stammered.

"Some motherfuckers just need to die." She hit the return button.

The little motor whirled and the metal hook, its three prongs still extended, ripped back through his chest. Blood and gore fountained everywhere. He managed a gurgle, dropped to his knees, and then went face down on the concrete.

She got to her feet wearily and clipped the grappling gun back to her belt. Then she stood over the body of the maniac who had tried to kill her multiple times, and kicked him in the ribs. Hard. To make sure he was dead.

CHAPTER TWENTY-EIGHT

Erin took in a long, slow breath. Her side ached, but she didn't care. She was tired, in pain and probably in big trouble, but Mr. Chaos was done, and she was going to take a second to savor that. She turned towards the front office, specifically the camera mounted on the corner of the roof, and nodded her head at it. A second later the front gate opened. Bernie ran in, while the rest of the crowd — well over three dozen now — applauded. That felt good. There was more to do still, but she'd taken down a homicidal killer and for the moment that was enough.

"Are you okay?" The reporter asked, still filming.

"Yes." She put her hand over the camera. "And shut it off, please."

"Alright." He shut off the phone and dropped it into his pocket. "I'm probably going to get in trouble for broadcasting that without a graphic content warning anyway."

She chuckled. "Seriously?"

"Oh my God. You have any idea how gross it was when that hook went through his chest?" He pantomimed the action. "And then back out again?"

She gestured to the blood on her suit. "Yeah. I was there."

"Yeah, right." He shifted nervously, searching for what to say next. He lowered his voice so only she could hear. "Your idea was brilliant. Since we couldn't use the information you got from his computer, tying the Mayor to Chaos will get the feds digging into his operation."

"I hope it was enough." She gingerly touched her ribs. "Otherwise he's going to get away with all of this."

"It was." He pulled his phone back out. "I got a text from a friend in the FBI who I had watching the live feed tonight. He was already interested, but as soon as Chaos pulled off his mask, my buddy recognized him as a mob enforcer wanted in four states. Hiring a guy like that is enough. The investigation will start first thing in the morning."

The sound of approaching sirens cut through her train of thought. "Shit. That might not be soon enough."

Bernie looked at the front gate and then back to her. "Get out of here. We'll buy you some time."

He ran back to the crowd. She looked back at the camera and held her right hand up, palm forward, fingers together with her thumb crossed over. Hopefully Mr. Johnson would understand. She turned and ran for her bike, tucked the Wishmaster into its holster, then swung her leg over and kicked the beast to life. As she gunned it towards the gate, the sirens were getting louder. Bernie shepherded the bystanders into a row between the cops and the facility, creating a wall of people to slow them down. She smiled broadly under her mask as she turned onto the road.

She shot over to Lovekin and then south to Hobsonway, into what the locals jokingly called hotel row — five cheap motels in a three-block area. Most of them were nationwide chains at least, but one wasn't. The Jade Inn. She'd picked that one for plan B because it was the only one that had a parking lot behind the building rather than in front. No one ever stayed there. She really had no idea how it was still in business.

The bike was coasting, and she killed the lights a block before turning into the lot. She glided around to the back, where she saw only one vehicle. It was an old dark-brown delivery van, one that had definitely seen better days. The rear doors were open and there was a metal ramp sticking out the back. Next to it was Robert, leaning back against the van and checking his watch. He looked up as she got closer and guided her right up the ramp and inside. He then flipped the ramp up into the van, and closed the doors.

Erin got off the bike and removed her helmet. She was tired of looking through the blood splattered on the visor.

Robert got behind the wheel and put the van into gear. "I assume everything went okay?"

"Yeah. I think so." She started removing her weapons. "Did Johnson tell you where to go?"

"Yup. Hang on." The van pulled forward with a jerk. "There's a duffle bag back there with a change of clothes. You can toss all your gear inside when you're done."

The van lumbered down Hobsonway, heading west out of town. She stripped out of her gear and into a pair of sweats and sneakers. All of it was new. "Do I thank you or Johnson for the outfit?"

"I picked it up for you. I wasn't going to rummage through your trailer to find something." He glanced over his shoulder. "I didn't want to stumble over something that would scar me for life."

"Don't worry, I keep all the bondage gear in my storage unit." There wasn't any passenger seat, so she squatted down next to him. "Any signs of a tail?"

"No. We're clear." He turned the van onto Mule Deer Ct. "We can drop it off down here. Johnson said he'll come get it in the morning. What did you do to get him to help you out so much?"

"Nothing. Other than taking a swan dive into his petunias." She chuckled. "And unlike you, he likes my ass."

He put his hands up. "It's not my fault I like a little more cushion."

They pulled into a trucking company's lot, and parked the van in with another half-dozen just like it. Robert got out and started walking to his own truck a few yards away. She paused, still inside, and looked back into the van. It felt weird leaving the suit and bike behind. Like she was suddenly naked and vulnerable. She wanted to scoop it up and take it home, but it was far better to stick to the plan. The Mayor would have the cops tearing up the city looking for the Sting, and the safest place would be as far from her gear as possible.

She got out of the van and locked the door. Robert was already in his truck, and had the engine running. She jogged over and got in, wincing at the pain in her side.

"You reinjure your ribs?" He asked, as the truck pulled away.

"No." She put her seatbelt on. "But Chaos beat them like a piñata."

"Okay. Let's get you home and I'll take a look at them." He turned and look at her seriously. "You really need to find a better class of boyfriend."

She cackled, and then grabbed her side. "Don't make me laugh."

Rock rummaged through his desk until he found the bottle of bourbon and a glass. His normal pull was two fingers, and a single cube to break the surface tension. This pour was far more generous. He skipped the ice and slugged back half of it in one gulp. He was pissed. At Chaos, for not doing his job and getting himself killed. At Wade, for not having captured the Sting by now. And at himself, for getting involved with all this shit in the first place.

Life had been so much easier before. Just take some kickbacks and a couple of bribes, and live the easy life. He'd been content with that. Then he'd hired Audrey, and he'd needed more. He wanted to impress her, lavish her in fine things, give her anything she wanted. He couldn't stand the idea of losing her. She never even asked for anything. Kept saying that all she wanted was him. That made him want to spoiler her even more.

Blythe had already been dying. All he had to do was help it on its way to the grave. He finished his bourbon and poured another, wondering how things had gone so wrong so fast. He wanted to blame it on that bitch in black and yellow, but honestly the whole thing had been a house of cards. Something had been almost bound to come knock it over at some point. But he'd refused to see the warning signs, and now it was all crumbling. She knew about the property purchases, Project Camelot, everything. It was just a matter of time before the feds showed up.

There was a knock on the door and Audrey leaned in. "Detective Furlong's here."

"Send him in."

She stepped back, and the detective bounced into the room. He seemed jittery, which meant that he was worried or anxious. "Any luck?"

He shook his head. "No. She's just vanished. My guys have looked everywhere."

The mayor stopped himself from snapping at him. Instead, he reached into his desk for a second glass, poured another stiff one and pushed it across the desk. "Sit down. We'll figure this out."

The detective sat, picked up the drink and sipped at it.

Rock took a deep breath to keep his calm. Freaking out would make nothing better. They could just sit and relax a moment while they waited for Spanky. The three of them should be able to figure out something, even if it meant leaving the country. All the excess money was in offshore accounts. It wasn't the big haul they wanted, but they could go live nicely in the Cayman Islands. He started imagining Audrey laying on the beach in a bikini.

Another knock on the door and she stepped in again. "Mr. Spinello's here."

"Thank you." He started looking for a third glass.

Spanky walked into the room without a word. He didn't take his usual seat, standing instead between the chairs. It took Rock a second to realize there was a gun in his hand. Before he could react, the mobster put the barrel against Wade's head and pulled the trigger. He turned the gun on Rock as the detective slumped over dead. The mayor groped urgently under his desk for his own gun, but it wasn't there. He looked over at Audrey who was still standing in the doorway. She blew him a kiss.

"That's my gun?" he asked. "You're going to make it look like we got into a fight? Wade took my gun from me, shot me and then himself? Murder suicide?"

With his free hand, Spanky put a toothpick in his mouth. "That's the general idea. It's nothing personal, you know. I actually like you. I hated that asshole," he nodded towards Wade's corpse, "but I like you."

"Our mysterious friend wants all loose ends tied up, then." Rock took a big swig of his bourbon, then looked towards Audrey. "Was she in on it the whole time?"

"Yeah. Sorry about that." The mobster shrugged. "The boss didn't think you were greedy enough to go along with it, so he sweetened your tooth for you. He's really good at reading people."

"So it seems." He starred at her for a moment, then back to the man with the gun. "Any chance you could let me go? I'll hop a plane for..."

"That's not going to happen." Spanky took aim. "Goodbye, Rock."

A week later, Erin was sitting in the little waiting room with its four folding chairs and fake ficus. She sat quietly, patiently. When Dr. Hertzberg opened the door, he almost seemed surprised to see here there, but covered it quickly and invited her in. She went in, took a seat and relaxed.

"How are you, Doctor?" she asked.

"I'm doing well. Thank you." He steepled his fingers in front of him. "How are *you* doing, Erin?"

She thought about it before answering. "I'm doing okay. I got a job. I have a place of my own. And I've made some new friends."

"That all sounds incredibly positive." He turned his computer towards her. It showed the Blythe Bulletin. "I've been keeping track of the other things you've been doing. Care to talk about that?"

A wide smile crossed her face. "Yeah. That has been very interesting. You were right about how much I needed to help people. To have a purpose. Everything I have now was a result of my stepping up and trying to help. I think I made a difference."

He leaned back in his chair. "What about the man you killed? Or the others that others who died that were involved. How do you feel about that?"

She weighed the question. "When I was a soldier, I took orders. As did my opponent. We'd try to kill each other, but only for a reason. You could argue whether it is ever a good reason, but it was war. You did your job and everything you could to keep yourself and your fellow soldiers alive. We tried to avoid killing unnecessarily, or hurting innocent bystanders. As much as we could. And both sides were fighting for something bigger than themselves."

"What about this masked killer? Was he different?"

"Very much so. His purpose was to kill. He did it because he enjoyed it." She looked the doctor in the eyes. "I gave him multiple opportunities to come out of it alive, because that's who I am. He pushed it to the death, because that's who he was. I won't lose any sleep over him."

Hertzberg smiled at his patient. "I'm very impressed. When I told you to keep doing what you were doing, I figured you'd stop a few muggings or something. Taking on a costumed criminal and toppling the local government was a bit more that I'd expected."

The both laughed.

"What can I say," she said. "I tend to do things in big ways."

"What's next?" He gestured towards her. "You came in here telling me about a job, a place to live, friends. Is it time to put the mask away and be just Erin for a while?"

She let out a big sigh. "That's the million-dollar question. I love all the new things in my life and they're important to me. But somewhere along the way, the people of this city became important to me too. Now they're without a mayor or chief detective. I figure I should probably keep an eye on things until Blythe gets back to normal. I mean, I don't plan on going out on nightly patrol or anything like that. But I could suit up if there is something serious to take care of. After that, I can quietly fade away and lead a normal life."

"You didn't read the headline on the Bulletin, did you?" He turned the computer back so he could read it out loud. "*On-Line Petition Started to Elect the Sting as Mayor of Blythe. Over 8,000 signatures already collected.*"

"What? Mayor?" Erin's eyes went wide. "You've got to be fucking kidding me."

Hertzberg watched as his patient left his office. The woman was full of surprises. He'd hated that he hadn't been able to get through to her. Between the PTSD, the alcohol and her self-sabotaging nature, he'd expected her to be another statistic long ago. But it turned out that she had an inner strength that kept her trying. And then, the last time he'd seen her, he'd seen the spark that he'd hoped to help grow. He really hadn't expected it to become a forest fire.

There was a knock on his other door.

"Come in."

Spanky walked in, toothpick tucked between his teeth. Audrey was close behind, and she pulled the door shut as she entered.

"You wanted to see us, Boss?" Spanky stood behind the guest chair, letting Audrey take a seat. "We bugging outta town?"

"No." He closed his laptop. "That won't be necessary. I had a session with Mr. West yesterday and helped guide him towards keeping Blythe as an option for Project: Camelot. I even eased him to the idea that he could do the greatest good in a city that had gone through the worst. He has quite the savior complex."

"I'm getting sick of this shithole," Audrey complained. "How much longer do I have to stay here?"

"A few more months will do it. But feel free to go take a week's bereavement in L.A." He stood and looked out his window. "I'm sure you're quite heartbroken over the loss of your lover."

"Yeah, right." She snorted.

"What about me?" Spanky shifted his toothpick to the other side. "You still want me to kill the Sting?"

Hertzberg looked out his window and watched as Erin pulled out of the lot. "No. There's a change of plans. We're actually going to help her."

Spanky looked confused. "Help her? To do what?"

The doctor turned back and smiled at them. "Why, to win an election of course."

ABOUT DAN WICKLINE

Dan Wickline is a published writer and photographer. Born in Norwalk, California, he currently resides in Los Angeles with his dog Artemis. Dan has written for Image Comics, IDW Publishing, Humanoids Publishing, Zenescope Entertainment, Avatar Press, Cellar Door Publishing and Moonstone Books. Recently Dan has written the re-launch of *Tales of Honor: Bred to Kill* for Top Cow and has also written a children's story entitled *The Mysterious Monkey of the Monarch Apartments* that is available on Amazon.com.

The creation of *Blythe: The Trailer Park Knight Rises* came about on a road trip to the Phoenix Comic Con in 2015. He was traveling with Lisa who looked around just after crossing back into California and asked where they were. Dan replied, "Blythe." To which Lisa said, "It's kind of a shithole." That comment lead Dan into thinking about how that could become the city motto and by the time he pulled into his driveway the concept for The Sting and her adventures was born.

If you would like more information about Dan Wickline, his work, or wish to contact him, please visit www.danwickline.com.

The Sting will return…

www.ingramcontent.com/pod-product-compliance
Lightning Source LLC
Chambersburg PA
CBHW070034260626
47159CB00005B/2036